S0-BSK-960

DATE DUE

AUG 2 4 2004		
GAYLORD		PRINTED IN U.S.A.

*Portrait
of a Man Unknown*

Portrait
of a Man
Unknown

a novel by
NATHALIE SARRAUTE

preface by Jean-Paul Sartre
translated by Maria Jolas

GEORGE BRAZILLER, INC.
New York, 1958

Theodore Lownik Library
Illinois Benedictine College
Lisle, Illinois 60532

843.9
S247pE

© 1958 George Braziller, Inc.

All rights reserved including the right of re-
production in whole or in part in any form.
Translated from *Portrait d'un Inconnu,* published in France by Gallimard.

Library of Congress Catalog Card Number:
58-7873
Manufactured in the United States of America

Published by George Braziller, Inc.
215 Fourth Avenue, New York 3, N. Y.

Preface

*O*ne of the most curious features of our literary epoch is the appearance, here and there, of penetrating and entirely negative works that may be called anti-novels. I should place in this category the works of Nabokov, those of Evelyn Waugh and, in a certain sense, Les Faux-Monnayeurs. By this I don't at all mean essays that attack the novel as a genre, such as Puissances du roman by Roger Caillois, which I should compare, with all due allowances, to Rousseau's Lettre sur les Spectacles. These anti-novels maintain the appearance and outlines of the ordinary novel; they are works of the imagination with fictitious characters, whose story they tell. But this is done only the better to deceive us; their aim is to make use of the novel in order to challenge the novel, to destroy it before our very eyes while seeming to construct it, to write the novel of a novel unwritten and unwritable, to create a type of fiction that will compare with the great compositions of Dostoievsky and Meredith much as Miro's canvas, "The Assassination of Painting," compares with the pictures of Rembrandt and Rubens. These curious and hard-to-classify works do not indicate weakness of the novel as a genre; all they show is that we live in a period of reflection and that the novel is reflecting on its own problems. Such is this book by Nathalie Sarraute: an anti-novel that reads like a detective story. In fact, it is a parody on the novel of "quest" into which the author has introduced a sort of impassioned amateur detective who becomes fascinated by a perfectly ordinary couple—an old father and a daughter who is no longer very young—spies on them, pursues them and occasionally sees through them, even at a distance, by virtue of a sort of thought transference, without ever knowing very well either what he is after or what they are. He doesn't find anything, or hardly anything, and he gives up his investigation as a result of a metamorphosis; just as though Agatha Christie's detective, on the verge of unmasking the villain, had himself suddenly turned criminal.

Nathalie Sarraute has a horror of the tricks of the novelist, even though they may be absolutely necessary. Is he "with," "behind," or "outside" his characters? And when he is behind them, doesn't he try to make us believe that he has remained either inside or outside? Through the fiction of this soul-detective, who knocks against the shell of these "enormous beetles" from the "outside," sensing dimly the *"inside" without actually touching it, Nathalie Sarraute seeks to safeguard her sincerity as a storyteller. She takes her characters neither from within nor from without, for the reason that we are, both for ourselves and for others, entirely within and without at the same time. The without is neutral ground, it is the* within *of ourselves that we should like to be for others and that others encourage us to be for ourselves. This is the realm of the* commonplace. *For this excellent word has several meanings. It designates, of course, our most hackneyed thoughts, inasmuch as these thoughts have become the meeting place of the community. It is here that each of us finds himself as well as the others. The commonplace belongs to everybody and it belongs to me; in me, it belongs to everybody, it is the presence of everybody in me. In its very essence it is generality; in order to appropriate it, an act is necessary, an act through which I shed my particularity in order to adhere to the general, in order to become generality. Not at all like everybody, but, to be exact, the* incarnation *of everybody. Through this eminently social type of adherence, I identify myself with* all *the others in the indistinguishableness of the universal. Nathalie Sarraute seems to distinguish three concentric spheres of generality: the sphere of character, the sphere of the moral commonplace, and the sphere of art—in particular, of the novel. If I pretend to be a rough diamond, like the father in the* Portrait of a Man Unknown, *I confine myself to the first sphere; if a father refuses to give money to his daughter, and I declare: "He ought to be ashamed of himself; and she's all he's got in the world . . . well, he can't take it with him, that's certain," then I take my position in the second sphere; and if I say*

of a young woman that she is a Tanagra, of a landscape that it is a Corot, or of a family chronicle that it's like something from Balzac, I am in the third. Immediately the others, who have easy access to these domains, approve and understand what I say; upon thinking over my attitude, my opinon, and my comparison, they give it sacred attributes. This is reassuring for others and reassuring for me, since I have taken refuge in this neutral and common zone which is neither entirely objective—since after all I am there as the result of a decree—nor entirely subjective—since I am accessible to everybody and everybody is at home there— but which might be called both subjectivity of the objective and objectivity of the subjective. And since I make no other claim, since I protest that I have nothing up my sleeve, I have the right, on this level, to chatter away, to grow excited, indignant even, to display my own person- ality, and even to be an "eccentric," that is to say, to bring commonplaces together in a hitherto unknown way; for there is even such a thing as the "hackneyed paradox." In other words, I am left the possibility of being subjective within the limits of objectivity, and the more subjective I am between these narrow frontiers, the more pleased peo- ple will be; because in this way I shall demonstrate that the subjective is nothing and that there is no reason to be afraid of it.

*In her first book, **Tropismes**, Nathalie Sarraute showed that women pass their lives in a sort of communion of the commonplace: "They were talking: 'They had the most terrible scenes and arguments, about nothing at all. All the same, I must say, he's the one I feel sorry for. How much? At least two million. And that's only what Aunt Josephine left. . . . Is that so . . . ? Well, I don't care what*

*you say, he won't marry her. What he needs is a wife who's
a good housekeeper, he doesn't even realize it himself. I
don't agree with you. Now, you listen to what I say. What
he needs is a wife who's a good housekeeper ... housekeeper
... housekeeper. ...' People had always told them so. That
was one thing they had always heard. They knew it: life,
love and the emotions, this was their domain, their very
own."*

*Here we have Heidegger's "babble," the "they," in other
words, the realm of inauthenticity. Doubtless too, many
writers, in passing, have brushed against the wall of inauthenticity, but I know of none who, quite deliberately,
has made it the subject of a book: inauthenticity being anything but novelistic. Most novelists, on the contrary, try to
persuade us that the world is made up of irreplaceable individuals, all exquisite, even the villains, all ardent, all
different. Nathalie Sarraute shows us the wall of inauthenticity rising on every side. But what is behind this wall?
As it happens, there's nothing, or rather almost nothing.
Vague attempts to flee something whose lurking presence
we sense dimly. Authenticity, that is, the real connection
with others, with oneself and with death, is suggested at
every turn, although remaining invisible. We feel it because we flee it. If we take a look, as the author invites us
to do, at what goes on inside people, we glimpse a moiling
of flabby, many-tentacled evasions: evasion through objects
which peacefully reflect the universal and the permanent;
evasion through daily occupations; evasion through petti-
ness. I know of few more impressive passages than the one
which shows us "the old man," winning a narrow victory
over the specter of death by hurrying, barefooted and in*

his nightshirt, to the kitchen, in order to make sure whether or not his daughter has stolen some soap. Nathalie Sarraute has a protoplasmic vision of our interior universe: roll away the stone of the commonplace and we find running discharges, slobberings, mucous; hesitant, amoeba-like movements. Her vocabulary is incomparably rich in suggesting the slow centrifugal creeping of these viscous, live solutions. "Like a sort of gluey slaver, their thought filtered into him, sticking to him, lining his insides." (Tropismes, p. *11.*) And here we have the pure woman-girl, "silent in the lamplight, resembling a delicate, gentle, underseas plant, entirely covered with live, sucking valves" (idem, p. *50*). The fact is that these groping, shamefaced evasions, which seek to remain nameless, are also relationships with others. Thus the sacred conversation, the ritualistic exchange of commonplaces, hides a "half-voiced conversation," in which the valves touch, lick and inhale one another. There is first a sense of uneasiness: if I suspect that you are not, quite simply, quite entirely, the commonplace that you are saying, all my flabby monsters are aroused; I am afraid: "She crouched on an arm of the chair, twisting her outstretched neck, her eyes bulging: 'Yes, yes, yes,' she said, nodding her head in punctuation of each phrase. She was frightening, mild and submissive, smoothed out flat, with only her eyes protruding. There was something distressing and disturbing about her, her very mildness was threatening. He felt that at any cost she must be pulled together and calmed, but that only someone with superhuman force would be able to do it. . . . He was afraid, on the verge of losing his head, and there wasn't a moment to spare for thinking things over. He started to

xii

talk, to talk without stopping, of anybody and anything, taking infinite pains (like a snake at the sound of a flute? like a bird in the presence of a boa constrictor? he no longer knew) he must hurry, hurry, without stopping, without a minute to lose, hurry, hurry, while there's still time, in order to restrain her, to placate her." (idem, p. 35.) Nathalie Sarraute's books are filled with these impressions of terror: people are talking, something is about to explode that will illuminate suddenly the glaucous depths of a soul, and each of us feels the crawling mire of his own. Then, no: the threat is removed, the danger is avoided, and the exchange of commonplaces begins again. Yet sometimes these commonplaces break down and a frightful protoplasmic nudity becomes apparent. "It seemed to them that their outlines were breaking up, stretching in every direction, their carapaces and armors seemed to be cracking on every side, they were naked, without protection, they were slipping, clasped to each other, they were going down as into the bottom of a well . . . down where they were going now, things seemed to wobble and sway as in an undersea landscape, at once distinct and unreal, like objects in a nightmare, or else they became swollen, took on strange proportions . . . a great flabby mass was weighing on her, crushing her . . . she tried clumsily to disengage herself a bit, she heard her own voice, a funny, too neutral-sounding voice. . . ." Nothing happens, in fact: nothing ever happens. With one accord, the speakers draw the curtain of generality before this temporary weakness. Thus we should not look in Nathalie Sarraute's book for what she does not want to give us: for her the human being is not a character, not first and foremost a story, nor even a network of habits, but a continual coming and going between the particular and the general. Sometimes the shell is empty. Suddenly there enters a "Monsieur Dumontet," who having knowingly rid himself of the particular, is reduced to a delightful, lively assemblage of generalities. Whereupon everybody takes a deep breath and hope returns: so it was possible, so it was still possible! A deathly calm accompanies him into the room.

These remarks have no other aim than to guide the reader through this difficult, excellent book; nor do they make any attempt to present its entire content. The best thing about Nathalie Sarraute is her stumbling, groping style, with its honesty and numerous misgivings, a style that approaches the object with reverent precautions, withdraws from it suddenly out of a sort of modesty, or through timidity before its complexity, then, when all is said and done, suddenly presents us with the drooling monster, almost without having touched it, through the magic of an image. Is this psychology? Perhaps Nathalie Sarraute, who is a great admirer of Dostoievsky, would like to have us believe that it is. For my part, I believe that by allowing us to sense an intangible authenticity, by showing us the constant coming and going from the particular to the general, by tenaciously depicting the reassuring, dreary world of the inauthentic, she has achieved a technique which makes it possible to attain, over and beyond the psychological, human reality in its very existence.

Jean - Paul Sartre

Portrait
of a Man Unknown

Once again I was not able to restrain myself, I couldn't help it; and although I knew that it was rash of me and that I risked a snubbing, tempted, I went a little too far.

First I tried, as I do sometimes, to take them unawares, using the gentle approach.

I began by being matter of fact and natural, in order not to frighten them. I asked them if they didn't sense, as I did, if occasionally they hadn't sensed something queer, a vague something that emanated from her and clung to them . . . but they snubbed me immediately, cutting me short, as usual, pretending not to understand: "She's a bit tiresome," they answered, "a bit of a bore . . ." I hung on: "Don't you think . . ." already my voice was giving out, it didn't sound true—in such moments one's voice never sounds true, it hesitates as it hunts around for a tone; having, in its confusion, mislaid its own, it tries to assume one that is plausible, well assured, respectable—in a voice that was too flat, too colorless, and which must have betrayed me, I tried to insist: "didn't they think, hadn't they occasionally sensed something that she exuded, something soft and gluey that stuck to them and inhaled them, without their knowing quite how, something they had to take hold of and tear off their skins, like a damp compress with a stale, sweetish odor. . . ." This was dangerous, going too far, which they detested . . . "something that sticks to you, permeates you, takes possession of you, worms itself in, something under the surface, perhaps, begging, demanding. . . ." I was out of my depth. But they pretended not to notice. They were determined we should remain on a normal, decent plane: "Yes, she seems to set great store by people's affection," they answered me like that in order to quiet me, to get it over with; they intended to call me to order. Or else—with them I can never help wondering—or else were they really, as they seemed to be, entirely unperceiving?

Yet one word from them, just one of those quick words that shoot forth from them and land in exactly the right place, like a boxer's blow, one word such as they occasionally know how to utter, would have kept me quiet for a while.

But when they are with me, this hardly ever happens, they are not sufficiently at ease.

In fact, it is in order to defend themselves against something ambiguous in me, something which, they realize vaguely, they should not share, it is precisely in order to amuse me and keep me at a distance, that they casually toss me these evasive opinions, that glance off without stunning, like light taps, and leave me unsatisfied.

For it to come out, they have to be by themselves, with everybody of the same mind, so that they understand one another right away and take it all quite naturally; they have to feel free and sure of their movements, two women who meet on the doorstep or in the stairway, carrying their market bags, in a hurry to go out, in a hurry to come in, preoccupied, and laughing with their shrill laughter, their thin, cutting laughter that goes right through me and rivets me to the floor above, afraid to breathe, avidly waiting: "He's a selfish old man," they're saying, "I always said so, selfish and close-fisted, people like that shouldn't be allowed to have children. As for her, she's just a crank. She doesn't know what she's doing. In my opinion she's more to be pitied than anything else, poor thing."

Then I realize that's it. I acknowledge their blinding perspicacity. It bowls me over; shining, convincing, absolutely irrefutable and terrible, it falls on me with a thud and lays me out flat as I listen, motionless, on the landing below, to their infallible judgment, their verdict.

But my wily efforts to get it out of them always end in failure. They won't let themselves be caught. Or perhaps with me—and without their knowing why—it simply doesn't come out. In any case, I'll never get anything out of them except what can be had by listening at keyholes, or the crumbs from their table.

All that was left for me to do, as always when I have

19

gone too far, was to try, through a painful effort, to detach myself from them and submit to their neglecting me and leaving me out of things; and then to wind up gracefully, with as much dignity as possible, and all due regard for appearances: "Well, somehow, I'm not so sure. To me she seems kind of queer (my voice—I can't help it—getting flatter and flatter, absolutely toneless), to me she seems to be rather strange, I don't know why." Then to try and leave, sort of offhandedly, like a person who suddenly remembers he's expected elsewhere, and who has noticed nothing (the way they have of saying: "No, I didn't see anything, what happened?" whenever I persist in my begging).

But I knew that my exit would not be a success; at such moments I am a little too conscious of my back. To leave like that always makes me look as though I had "cut and run."

Of course I know that whenever I want to I can always make up for it with the others, with the people in whose company I feel warmth and intimacy; the ones who never indulge in snubbing and are easy to approach. They're the kind that surely never exclude anyone, never put anyone in his place. They probably wouldn't know how to set about it.

They are curiously passive and, as it were, a bit inert. They greet me with a smile that is always slightly ironic and a little too friendly: they seem to have been waiting for me with infinite modesty and patience, even with a curious humility towards me.

With them I can let myself go. Nothing will ever seem to them to be improper, "literary" or artificial. They will understand right away. I can approach them, and without putting out any subtle feelers, can take all the preliminary stages with one leap, all the comparisons with damp compresses and sweetish odors, with everything that clings, adheres to you, permeates you, draws you to it without your knowing it (they feel that right away, they know it perfectly well; all these expressions which seem obscure and vaguely indecent to the others are a matter of everyday speech between them and me, technical terms, familiar to the initiated). As I gain in courage, I can take it out of my pocket and show them—they won't be the least surprised —the paper, the envelope, the proof I have kept, across which spreads her mark (like tracks left in the snow by the claws of a furtive animal): first of all the huge "M," written with sloppy offhandedness, a lopsided, intentionally vulgar, sprawling affair, that I recognize as hers, and then the enormous rigid downstroke, hard and shockingly aggressive, that cuts through the address and nearly across the entire envelope, like an intolerable challenge, that attacks me and literally makes me sick. . . . I know I can show it to them and that they will answer me on this one special point, without asking any embarrassing questions, with the detached, dignified manner of an expert giving his opinion on documents in a file that does not concern him personally.

With all my might I pray they won't see anything, that they will blame me, that they will put me in the wrong and the others in the right, that they will hand back the envelope after a somewhat careless, surprised and slightly disapproving inspection: "No, I see nothing. There doesn't seem to me to be anything in particular. . . . It's really of no interest. . . ."

Just as in my childhood I was afraid, terribly afraid (it

was a feeling of anguish and bewilderment) when strangers took my side against my parents and tried to console me for having been unjustly scolded, when I should have a thousand times preferred, in the face of all justice and all evidence, that they had blamed me, so that everything could have been normal and decent and I could have had, like other children, real parents one would like to obey, and in whom one could feel confidence (it's funny how these early fits of the confused, almost forgotten anguish of our childhood, which we thought were cured, suddenly return, with exactly the same intensity, in moments of weakness, or lowered resistance . . . regression to the stage of infantilism, I believe is how the psychiatrists must call it), now, too, I should like them to blame me, to put me in the wrong and the others in the right, those others who don't understand, who will have none of me; I should like them not to force me to take sides against them, but to drive me back to them, allowing me to become subject to their will, as I still want to do, to have confidence in them—so that everything may be on a normal, decent plane.

But as was to be expected, they saw it right away: "Those M's . . . very strange. And, in fact, they're quite characteristic . . . both aggressive—the downstroke is extraordinary . . ." they are smiling . . . "brutally aggressive, and sprawling. Even the pothooks at the top, if looked at closely, show a special sort of sloppiness that is somewhat bantering and provocative." They know a lot. But in the face of all evidence, I nevertheless continue to have a vague hope. I grow insistent: "Really, so you think so too? For that matter, you know her well, unless I'm mistaken? And him too? Frankly, what is your impression?"

22

They don't seem surprised by my insistence. Generously, and without anything to be gained for them by it—I realize that, just now, this is not what interests them—they are willing to do what they can: "Yes, I remember. I went to see them. That was quite a while ago. I seem to recall that they lived in an old apartment with antiquated furniture, yellow hangings, sash curtains, all very lower middle class, and probably looking on a dark courtyard. One could easily imagine vague things swarming in the corners, threatening creatures, you know what I mean . . . waiting and watching. Because of her somewhat oversized head, she reminded one of a huge mushroom that had grown up in the dark. The general effect was rather like something out of Julian Green or Mauriac." They smile: "She must have loved that nice, big Malempia* of theirs. . . ."

I have the impression that they are sneering; they seem delighted to show me that they, too, know this. . . . With this word I feel they have taken a sudden leap that brings them closer to me. They notice that I have understood immediately, only too much so . . . and that I have shrunk back very slightly. They begin to laugh: "They must have enjoyed that, she and the old man, shut up in there, the two of them, with no desire to leave, breathing in their own smelly atmosphere, all snug and warm in their nice, big Malempia." This word seems to have a slightly titillating effect on them, to excite them; it is as though it had opened up something in them, touched off a spring; something is about to start, their eyes begin to shine—the tall, gaunt

* From *La Séquestrée de Poitiers*, by André Gide, the story of a victim of lifelong illegal confinement who begs to be allowed to return to the unbelievably filthy room from which she has been rescued, to which she refers by the invented name, "Malempia."

young man who looks like a circus freak leans back, his long fingers twined about his bony knee, his skinny legs begin to twist, his lip curls over his prominent eye teeth that are like two little fangs—he all but sniffs. He leans towards me: "I have even heard. . . ." By now I feel them very close to me, right up against me, I don't quite take in what they are whispering in my ear . . . it is as though they were passing something over my face, as gently and delicately as possible, in order not to frighten me, hardly touching the down of my skin which they brush back with their soft fingertips, ever so lightly, hardly breathing. . . . "I have even heard it said . . . people have told me that the old man gets up at night . . . he never sleeps at night . . . he makes her get up, too . . . he is always suspecting her of something. . . ." They press a little harder . . . "At night he makes her count with him the soiled dish towels drying in the kitchen and the number of burnt matches . . . he collects all the old newspapers. . . ." By now I feel that they are withholding nothing, they continue, unrestrained . . . "in fact, his wife died from neglect. . . . It seems he made his children wear black underclothes . . . to save laundry. Can't you just see that now, all of them dressed in black, lying there in their beds, in the corner of one of those dark rooms. . . ." They laugh delightedly, with growing excitement seizing upon bits of stupid gossip, recollections of old news items, thick "slices of life" painted in raw, too crude colors, absolutely unworthy of them and of me, which they toss at me; by now, satisfied with just anything, they seize on anything at all and smear me with it, they grasp hold of me any way, they grasp the three of us, me, her and the old man, they hold us all together, squeezed one against the other, they press us tightly one against the other, they press against us, they clasp us to them.

The tall, gaunt young man closes his eyes, stretches his skinny neck further and further backwards, like a drinking duck; one can hear the faint flutter of his tongue, recovering his saliva, as he adds further details. He laughs with a grating laughter, that catches hold of you from below and drags you along. . . .

This time, as almost always when things have gone a little too far, I have the impression of having "touched bottom"—an expression I often use: I have a certain number of these, landmarks such as are probably possessed by all those who, like myself, drift timorously in the half-light of what is poetically termed "the inner landscape"—"I touched bottom," this always calms me somewhat for the moment, forces me to pull myself together; it always seems to me, when I have said that to myself, that now my two feet have pushed off from the bottom with all the strength I have left, and that I am coming up again. . . .

This time I felt that it was the moment to come up again, to call a halt to a game that had gone too far. So I resorted once more to another of my devices—one I employ in desperate cases, similar to the tricks that doctors discover empirically and sometimes recommend as a last resort to their "neuropaths," such as, to practice smiling every day in front of a mirror so that, with patient repetition, this artificial grin may induce gaiety: I can almost hear them, with that air of mealy-mouthed solidarity of theirs, saying: "When we are unfortunate enough not to be able to walk straight, it's better, don't you agree, to walk backwards, if by so doing we can reach our goal? Whatever people may say, putting the cart before the horse sometimes gives good results. . . ." So I, too, decided to use one of my tricks, somewhat similar to that one, the result of painful experimenting, which sometimes gives good results.

I went out into the street. I realize that the impression the streets in my neighborhood make on me is unreliable. I am afraid of their rather saccharine quietude. The house fronts look strangely inert. On the public squares, between the big corner buildings, are wan little gravel plots, surrounded with a box hedge inside a protective, waist-high black grating. This hedge always makes me think of the fringe of beard that they say grows so thickly on corpses. I know quite well that impressions of this kind have probably been analyzed and catalogued long before now, along with other morbid symptoms: I can see it perfectly in one of those psychiatric handbooks in which the patient is decked out for convenience's sake with a familiar, occasionally rather ridiculous name, such as Octave or Jules. Or simply Oct. M., aged 35.

In his "empty" or "bad bad" periods, Oct. M., 35, keeps saying that everything seems to be dead. The houses, the streets, even the air, seem to him to be dead: "Everywhere you go, you feel dead childhoods. No childhood memories here. Nobody has any. They fade and die as soon as they form. They never seem to succeed in getting a grip on these pavements, or on these lifeless house fronts. And the people, the women and the old men, sitting motionless on the benches, in the little plots, look as if they were in a state of decomposition." I can see this perfectly. In fact I must have seen it in almost those very words in a psychiatric handbook. But I'm not ashamed of that. I'm not trying to be original. I didn't start out to cultivate my own personal sensations, but to get something I want more than I can say—"the other view"; the one not mentioned in the medical books, for the reason that it is so natural, so innocuous and familiar; the one that Octave or Jules also sees in his lucid moments, during his periods of calm.

There's a trick you can use to get it, if you aren't lucky enough to get it spontaneously, as a matter of course. A sort of sleight-of-hand rather similar to the exercises required for solving certain puzzles, or those pictures composed of black and white diamonds so cleverly combined that they form two superimposed geometrical drawings; the game consists of a sort of visual gymnastics: you detach, very gently, one of the drawings, move it a bit, push it back, and then you bring the other one forward. With a little practice, a certain dexterity can be acquired which makes it possible to switch very quickly from one drawing to the other, to see first one, then the other, at will.

Here in these little streets, when I walk about all alone,

on one of my good days, I occasionally succeed, more easily than elsewhere, in accomplishing a rather similar sleight-of-hand trick in order to get the "other" view.

To do this, I am not obliged, as some may think, to try to come closer to things, to make an effort to wheedle them into being innocuous and familiar—I never succeed in that; on the contrary, I have to get as far away from them as possible, keep them at arm's length, take a rather remote, aloof attitude and treat them as strangers. A stranger walking in a strange city. Then, as one often does in strange cities, apply to things I see, and keep in the foreground, remembered images, literary or otherwise, recollections of pictures or even of postcards like those that have written on the back: Paris, Banks of the Seine, A Public Square.

There is nothing better for bringing the other view back into the foreground. Houses, streets, public squares, all lose their inert, strange, vaguely threatening aspect. Like protographs slipped under the lens of a stereoscope, they seem to come alive, assuming relief and warmer coloring.

That day, everything went well. I succeeded rather quickly. It was one of my good days. I was on the up-grade. I was very sure of myself and rather calm. I had already begun to feel the relaxation, the rather special buoyancy, indulgence and light-heartedness that I feel on a journey. The streets began to come to life. More and more they assumed the rather sad, tender charm of Utrillo's little streets. The big corner buildings seemed to sway gently in the gray air. It was as though a fine jet, a slender thread of life, ran the length of their trembling edges.

I made so bold as to go and sit down in one of the plots, in an open square not far from where I lived. In one

30

corner, near the box hedge, a tree covered with white flowers stood out against a dark wall, with a certain vividness, almost alive, as it might have looked in a square in Haarlem or in Bruges. With the liberty and sort of off-handed naïveté of a foreigner I asked a little old woman sitting next me on the bench if she knew the name of that tree. Her eyes lighted up with an expression of tenderness—it was as though she had just been thinking about it herself: "I believe it's a whitebeam," she replied. And everything became really very gentle and calm. I felt at ease. I had been entirely successful. As I always do in my good moments, I said over to myself my favorite proverbs: Heaven helps him who helps himself ("the wisdom of the people"); or, the one I particularly like—I believe it's always quoted in connection with marriage, but I like to apply it to "life": It's like a Spanish inn, you find in it only what you bring to it. Instead of the sinister little old men or the "old pencil woman" who haunted the unfortunate Malte Laurids Brigge in places that were probably very similar to this one, I had succeeded, by knowing how to go about it—you have to be able to show them that you see them from the good side and have confidence in them—in finding, on this Utrillo-like square, this little old woman sitting beside me, murmuring very gently and looking at the white tree.

Small wonder that in this gently relaxed mood I had not the faintest presentiment. Not a trace of the slight disquiet, the vague excitement—a mixture of fear and eager expectancy—which I always feel before even noticing them. It is doubtless this which often gives me the impression that it is I who arouse them, who call them forth. It has sometimes happened that during an entire theatrical performance I have felt their presence in the audience without seeing them. It was only on the way out that suddenly, just as they disappeared around a turn in the stairway, I would catch sight of the furtive outline of their backs or, reflected in a mirror, in the crowd streaming in front of me, the nape of their necks. Certain apparently insignificant details of their appearance, of their general get-up, catch and hold my eye immediately—like a harpoon that strikes deep and pulls.

Now I hardly felt anything, a slight, very much deadened shock at the moment when I saw her outlined in the latticed gate of the square. But that was enough. I stood up right away. I crossed the square very quickly, almost running; there was no time to lose, I had to catch up with her, see her turn around, I had to make sure, at whatever cost, that everything was still innocuous and natural, that everything was all right. . . . And yet it is the kind of thing I never succeed at—I know it quite well, I never succeed when I try to come close either to people or to things, or when I try to curry favor. I must keep my distance—but I couldn't stop myself, I felt already the attraction they still have for me, like a rush of air that draws everything along, a sort of dizziness, a plunge into the void. . . .

She had seen me. There was no doubt about it. For she too has a sort of supernatural flair for things. She feels this: she feels me behind her, and certainly, too, when I follow her in the crowd after the theatre, she feels my eyes on her back, in the mirror. She had had a presentiment of my presence, she had noticed my head right away, emerging above the box hedge on the bench beside the petrified little old people, or perhaps, just between the bars of the fence, the outline of my crossed legs.

She had seen that without even turning her head, out of the corner of one eye, without looking my way; she hadn't needed to look. Now she begins to walk a little faster, not too fast, however, she's afraid to attract my attention as she steps up onto the pavement; I recognize quite well the rather special way she swings her arm, holding on to the child's schoolbag she always carries by way of a purse. Doubtless for her too it is against the rules of the game, it is entirely unlikely that I should follow her or even dare to speak to her at this moment. And certainly she must have her own infallible presentiments and signs, with regard to me. I am so keyed up . . . so emotionally stirred . . . a very special sensuousness, extremely gentle and at the same time frightening and ambiguous (as always, this mixture of attraction and fear) urges me on, quick, quick, at the second when I lay my hand on her shoulder and call her by name, I couldn't have waited another minute. She has seen me: that is now certain. Otherwise she would have turned around when she felt me so close behind her, when I was about to touch her.

She gave a sort of jump to one side—that jump to one side, with her behind flattened out like a hyena's, is exactly what I had dreaded—and turned around. Her eyes, like the eyes of a hyena, fled mine. I smiled a saccharine smile, as if nothing had happened, and tried to continue to play the game: "Hello, how are you? I caught a glimpse of you . . . I was sitting there on a bench sunning myself, when I

33

noticed you in the gateway of the square. . . ." She made no reply, her eyes rolled from side to side like two frantic marbles about to run out of their groove; it was almost audible, the way I bowed and scraped in my efforts to approach her and win her over: "Everything is so lovely just now, don't you think? Every year in the spring, even though we sense that we're growing older we feel again. . . ." But she won't be taken in. She sees my game right away, as well as the thing that exists between us, which I try to hide. I have her cornered; she stands there without moving; all she does is to wriggle a bit. I have the impression that she is trembling ever so slightly, that she approves of what I am saying, merely punctuating each of my sentences docilely with a slight whistle, an *ee-ye-es* that makes one think of the last gulps of a little girl allowing herself to be consoled after a fit of sobbing. There is something almost touching in her passivity, in her awkwardness, that keeps her from answering in the same vein; in comparison with myself—I see it sort of vaguely—there is something about it that even approaches purity. But I can't let go, I try to come a bit closer still: "It's wonderful, don't you think so, this sort of exquisite nostalgia which, in spite of age, certain spring evenings bring back? The Paris trees . . . the little squares. . . ." She agrees, smiling her contracted smile. . . . Finally she makes up her mind, her eyes take on a hunted look, she squirms more than ever and holds out the tips of her bony fingers; her voice becomes tiny, all but strangled: "I believe it's quite late, I'm a bit late, I think I ought to run" (there's that word "run," which she always uses; an oozing, cowardly word, but I've no time to linger over it, no, not now). I have a feeling of unbearable anguish, a chill, as though a gaping hole had opened up inside me, I have to make an effort not to pursue her, not to call her back, to speak to her once more, to do just anything, to beg her: perhaps it's still not too late, perhaps there is yet time to make amends. . . . But she has run. I see her back, flattened as though by the wind, turning the corner of the street: this is a dodge—it's not her direction, she is going out of her way to escape me as quickly as possible, to flee my eye.

She must be walking very fast; she had been wasting her time clowning there with me, now she will have to make it up; she begins to hurry, there is something obstinate and avid, something blind and relentless in the way she advances in the right direction, cutting across the streets, her back still flattened out as though threatened by a kick from behind, her long thin legs out in front.

It would undoubtedly amuse her, if she still has time to think about me, it would amuse her, now that she feels free and that I no longer frighten her, to know that I am still following her, still spying on her. . . . She goes up the dark, silent stairway, with its wall covering of imitation tooled leather. She feels in her bag for the key, quick, she has no time to lose, it's late, and, besides, she probably feels, as I did just now, a sort of trembling, a painful and pleasurable emotion which swells and grows. . . . To the right of the entrance, leading to the study, is the narrow corridor, covered with a yellow-bordered, dingy gray paper. Here, emanating from the lavatory, there is always a kind of vague odor of dust and urine, probably whiffs from the toilet. . . . She would surely taunt me now, if she had time: "So that's it? La Bonifas? Adrienne Mesurat? That's it? Sinister rooms looking out on gloomy courtyards? The way they uncoil like serpents in the dark?" She would smile, surely, as the others did, when they answered me with their funny little smile, when they teased and tickled me, when they tried to get me excited about their nice big Malempia. Whatever I may do, she is perfectly calm. I can hang on like a stubborn mongrel that won't let go. All I'll ever succeed in tearing off is a very tiny piece of living substance. . . .

He is there, ensconced in his study, like a huge spider, watching and waiting; ponderous, motionless; he appears to be all hunched over; he's biding his time. He straightens up as soon as he hears, in the entrance, her exaggeratedly soft voice, the voice she always uses when she speaks to the maid, the same she had used with me a little while before, a tiny, toneless voice, all choked up. He rushes across the room and, turning his back to the door, hurries to take his place in front of the mantelpiece, where he pretends to be sorting some papers. Like her, he is given to these furtive gestures, these last-minute preparations, and rapid tidyings-up: occasionally he has even been caught hastily composing his facial expression, before the door opens.

She remains in the doorway. . . . And almost immediately it flares up between them . . . their snakelike coilings and uncoilings. . . . But I feel I'm beginning to lose touch, they've got the upper hand, they drop me en route, I let go. . . . She must be asking for something, he refuses, she insists. It's almost sure to be a question of money. . . . I recall the gaunt young man, who looks like a circus freak,

leaning towards me: "Julian Green . . . ? Or Mauriac . . . ?
They say he gets up at night, collects old newspapers. . . ."
They would have a good laugh at me now. . . . There must
be a lot of noise, accompanied by blows and shouts. . . .
Followed by silence. Then a few slammed doors. An odor
of valerian in the narrow corridor. . . . It's all over. . . .
There she is already, eyes and cheeks still red. She strides
hurriedly along, her back humble and furtive, as usual.
Only her stretched-out neck is aggressively stiff, and her
head looks like a clenched fist: "Cantankerous brute," she
mutters.

She is inscrutable now, walled in on every side, much
stronger than a while ago. She wouldn't see me, she
wouldn't even notice me, this time, if I were to hide, as I
sometimes do, under the porch across the way, my eyes
glued to the glass panels of the double doors that gleam like
black water at the back of the vestibule, waiting to see them
appear. Or perhaps she would just give me a sidewise
glance, the amused look of a fellow conspirator, if by any
chance she were to notice me hiding there, waiting.

Nothing amuses them so much, when they're in their
more cheerful moods, and are feeling quite sure of themselves, as little weaknesses of this kind in me. Sometimes
they find them very amusing. Then they grow playful.
Even give me a little nip here and there, just to tease me,
and I always let them do it.

I have a recollection of him, one time. . . . He's much
cleverer than she is at that kind of game. . . . Sometimes
quite cunning, even. I had passed him on the stairs. He had

37

recognized me right away, and burst into his falsely good-natured laughter: "Well, well, so it's you, is it? I wondered if it was you, coming up so fast. . . . Always in a hurry, eh? Where are you bound for, at such a pace? Always something on your mind, haven't you? Always worrying?" I get out of my depth with him right away, replying with constraint, slightly spluttering, and with a smile that quickly becomes shamefaced, embarrassed. With his subtle flair he scents vaguely something in me, a frightened little animal that trembles and cowers deep down inside. He feels around, the way one pokes with the tip of an iron rod in order to rout out a crab from its hole in the rock; to begin with, perhaps, a bit at random: "Well, well, still making plans this year? Traveling? Corsica? Italy? Eh?" He feels something moving, he comes closer, presses hard. His great bloated mass bears down on me, flattening me against the wall: "Greece? The Parthenon? Eh? The Parthenon? Museums? The Eleusinian Mysteries? Have you been to Eleusis? Art? Florence? Pictures? The Uffizi? You've seen all that? Eh?"

I draw back, shrinking against the wall, my eyes lowered . . . Now he feels he has got it; driving home the spike, he gives a direct stab, laughing: "And Sceaux? How about that? Sceaux-Robinson, eh? Have you been there?" The frightened little animal, cowering deep down inside, has stopped moving—he's pinned it down. . . . "How about Bagneux? That doesn't tempt you? Or Suresnes? That doesn't tempt you either, eh? Bagneux? Sceaux-Robinson?" He's enjoying himself hugely. Finally he lets me go: either he feels sorry for me or perhaps he's too disgusted with me, or else he's got what he wanted, he's calmed down, or perhaps he wants to wind up pleasantly, covering up his tracks —it's like him. . . . He draws away a bit, looking into the distance, his manner suddenly becomes serious, this is his rather soulful, sincere manner, which is part of his charm: "Yes, yes, those are all pleasant memories for me, Suresnes . . . the bridge at St. Cloud . . . I still go there sometimes. I remember the old days, on Sunday afternoons, you weren't born then, eh . . . ?" He breaks out into his good-natured, jovial laughter. He slaps me heartily on the back. . . . I almost begin to doubt. . . . What had I been thinking about? I'm even taken in. I agree heartily, and he leaves me, delighted, after a final resounding, friendly, patronizing slap on the back.

It's not until a moment later, when he has already gone, that, without being able to put my finger on it, I have a vague sense of uneasiness, like a slight itching which I scratch here and there, or a burning, like the sensation left by nettles.

Thus, from time to time, they like to amuse themselves at my expense, in their own insidious, subtle way. They are not afraid of me. It rarely happens that I succeed in taking them by surprise as I did her just now, on the square, when I caught her on the run, at a moment when she didn't expect it, and she gave her jump to one side and squirmed under my glance, weak and defenseless as a hermit crab just taken out of its shell. But it wasn't for long. She pulled herself together very quickly, as soon as she had turned the corner; she climbed rapidly back into her shell, the armor in which she feels safe from harm.

She is well protected, unassailable, shut in, watched over on every side. . . . Nobody can broach her. Nobody identifies her when she walks by with her constricted expression, looking straight ahead with hard, bulging eyes and the stubborn precision of an insect.

Nor does anybody identify all those others in the streets who, like her, go slinking along beside the walls, avid and obstinate.

They wait behind doors. They ring. The family neurotic, curled up at the foot of the bed, ensconced at the far end of his room which looks out on a damp little courtyard, hears their ring. He had been waiting for it, his eyes glued to the clock: a sharp, short ring which never comes late, but rather on the early side, always inclined to be five minutes ahead of time. He recognizes it right away: furtive, slightly urgent and already aggressive, relentless. A sharp, cold little ring, which is repeated at regular, calmly calculated intervals, as often as is needed to get an answer.

There they stand behind the door. Waiting. He feels them unfolding, creeping insidiously towards him. They grope about. They aim their suckers towards the sensitive, vital spot in him, knowing exactly where it is.

Except for him, nobody sees them standing ponderously in the doorways, like pot-bellied tumbler dolls weighted down with lead, which always straighten up again if laid flat, thrown to the ground or knocked over. They always straighten up again. No matter whether you scratch or bite them, throw them out shouting, shake them or hurl them downstairs—they get up again, a little sore, give a pat to the pleats in their skirts, and back they come.

Nobody identifies them as they walk past, very proper, with trim hat and gloves. They refasten their gloves carefully in the vestibule before ringing the door bell. On summer afternoons, the concierges, seated in the doorways to get a bit of fresh air, watch them walk by: grandmothers who are not allowed to see their grandchildren as often as they should, daughters who go to see their old fathers at least twice a week, all kinds of neglected women, mal-treated women, who have come to explain their case.

Formerly, when they were still quite young, much less resistant and less robust, a trained eye would have been able to pick them out—already avid and ponderous, already weighted down with lead—watching and waiting, on the plush chairs at the dancing class, or in ballrooms, or in the casinos at fashionable resorts, seated beside their parents, around little tables at tea time. A sort of thick, acrid substance exuded from them like sweat or grease. All kinds of creeping, gnawing little desires uncoiled in them like tiny snakes, nests of vipers, worms: hidden, corrosive desires, somewhat like those of Madame Bovary. They watched smartly dressed young men who also strongly resembled those Madame Bovary had noticed in the ballrooms of her day, gliding past over polished floors. These young men had the same manner, the same airy, supple way of holding their heads; they, too, let their indifferent glance rove at random; they had the same expression of aloof, rather dull-witted satisfaction. The tentacles that issued already from the girls, the little sucking, groping valves, hardly grazed them. They felt, at the most, a sort of tickling, as though gossamer threads had brushed them, clinging to their clothes, threads which they shed without being aware of them, as they went on their way. The girls watched them glide close by, unseeing, staring into space with their fashionably expressionless, cold fisheyes, moving unerringly away, guided by mysterious, indeterminable currents.

Later, in their beds at night, the damsels would weep and wring their hands, trying to understand, imploring Providence. . . .

But little by little they had gained experience and assurance. With the almost imperceptible, delicate movements of a bird, the infallible instinct that causes it to sort out exactly what is needed to build its nest, they had succeeded, little by little, in picking up, here and there, from everything that came to hand, bits and scraps which they had put together to build themselves a soft little nest, within which they stayed, well protected, watched over on every side, well sheltered.

It was extraordinary to see with what rapidity, skill and voracious tenacity they caught on the wing, managed to extract from everything, books, plays, films, a quite unimportant conversation, a random phrase, a proverb, a song, pictures, chromos—*Childhood, Maternity, Pastoral Scenes, The Joys of Home,* or even subway posters and advertisements, the principles laid down by manufacturers of soap powders and face creams ("How to hold a husband . . ."), the advice of Aunt Annie or Father Soury—it was extraordinary to see how unfailingly, among all the things that came to hand, they seized upon exactly what was needed to spin their cocoon, their impermeable covering, to fashion this armor in which later on, under the kindly eye of the concierges, they went forth—amid general encouragement, unconquerable, calm and assured: grandmothers, daughters, maltreated women, mothers—standing at doors, pressing with all their weight against doors, like heavy battering rams.

Now and then, when I have been seated next to them at the theatre, without looking at them, while they listened motionless and as though turned to stone beside me, I have sensed the trail left across the entire audience in the wake of the images emanating from the stage or from the screen, images that settle on them like steel filings on a magnetic surface; I longed to rise, to intervene and check these images in their flight, to turn them aside; but they flowed with an irresistible force, straight from the screen onto the women; they clung to them; and I felt the women close beside me, in the darkness of the hall, motionless, silent and voracious, spinning these images into an object destined for their own use.

I must have seemed somewhat queer; I realized this by the slightly astonished, amused way the passers-by looked at me. I was walking very fast, almost running, as sometimes happens in my moments of excitement, when I give in to digressions of this kind, to my "visions," as I like pompously to call them. I must have been smiling to myself, for someone who brushed me in passing whispered shrilly: "Doesn't he look pleased. . . ."

I was very pleased indeed, very satisfied. I was running, flying even, across the boulevard, straight to the little café where I knew I could find him at that hour, I was very anxious to see him, to let him know right away, I had to strike while the iron was hot, no time to lose. . . . And there

43

he was, at our usual table in one of the back rooms; he was waiting for me, my old pal, my *alter ego,* as we used to call each other, my old companion in crime.

By the gleam in his half-closed eyes, I could tell that he had understood right away, from the moment he saw me, that this would be one of our good days, that I had a juicy morsel for him. He knows me. He's been used to my tricks for a long time now. I've trained him. Our collusion dates from the time when we used to amuse ourselves, apart from the others, in a corner of the schoolyard, by delicately carving into little pieces our schoolmates, our teachers, our parents, our parents' friends, even the shopkeepers in our neighborhood, whom we fell back on when the supply began to dwindle. Since then, in his spare time, I've taken him in training. For that matter, he has real talent. At the time of our schoolboy frolics, his department was mimicry. He was excellent. I promised him that he would be a great actor. We supplemented each other very well; the preliminary carving helped him develop niceties, expressions and intonations of great subtlety. All he does now is to tinker about in his spare time, urged on by me, happy enough if the opportunity arises to be able to lend me a hand. But what I particularly like about him is that he continues to believe in me, as he did in the days when I used to strut cockily about the schoolyard, as though nothing had changed and he had never noticed what I've come to since.

My back to the mirror, I slide in beside him on the oilcloth-covered bench. The small back room is warm and filled with smoke. Here we are, as in the old days, seated close together, apart from all the others.

I have the delicious, cozy sensation of someone about to step into a warm bath. I am in no hurry. I am relishing the situation. He waits patiently. At last, I gently take the plunge. . . . "You know, I saw her, I saw her again; she appeared on the scene suddenly, when I was not expecting it, while I was lounging on a bench in a public square. It was just as always, like characters out of Pirandello. So much so, this time, that I almost didn't believe it. I ran after her, of course, I couldn't help it, I caught up with her, she was frightened, she wasn't prepared for it, she was literally trembling. . . . You know how they are: how frightened they get . . . the way they tremble and twitch, their sense of shame . . . one doesn't dare look them in the eye . . . you remember . . . the-people-who-make-you-squirm? When she turned around she jumped, with her behind flattened out, exactly the way a hyena jumps; something awful. . . ." I have the impression that from beneath his lowered lids, a glance of discerning approbation flows over me like a deliciously warm current. . . . "But afterwards, as soon as she got away, I saw suddenly, by the expression of her back, something that struck me, something greedy and ponderous. A sort of frightening determination. . . . She was going to see the old gentleman, that's certain. Trampling everything down in her path. A blind, relentless force. A real battering ram. It *happened* then. . . ." He smiled: "So it's still there, is it? It still gets you? You remember that time we laughed so hard. . . . We had been supposing that one day I should be strolling about a museum or at an exhibition, and that suddenly I should see on the wall, beside the *Portrait of Madame X* or the *Girl with Parrot*, something which I could recognize immediately, ten yards away, as having been done by you, some-thing that unquestionably bore your signature, your mark. . . ." He laughed: "Beside the *Girl with Fan,* an exquisite portrait, painted by you, what was it you called it . . . ? Oh yes. . . . That was very like you . . . *Hypersensitive Girl with. . . ."* It was true, how could I have forgotten it, now it came back to me, *Hypersensitive Girl, Cliché-fed.* . . . Her name. . . . It was the one I had given her back in the old days. . . . It was true. . . . My discoveries are always like that. . . . More often than not that's how my moments of triumph and beatitude end: by mistaking long-discarded things for fresh discoveries . . . by forever going over old ground. . . .

But I refused to be put off; "Listen, all joking aside, this time I think I've got it, I think I'm on the right track. . . ." I told him everything: the sucker-lined ghouls waiting behind doors, the battering rams, the tumbler dolls, the old-style virgins, wallflowers wilting on ballroom chairs, thin-lipped grandmothers rebuttoning their gloves before ringing, grubs spinning their cliché cocoons in dark movie houses. . . . I felt that he didn't like this, but I was de-termined to convince him, I kept on: "I can tell you, it's as though I saw them now: all their eddies and quakings and tremblings, the swarms of little shameful, creeping de-sires inside them, what we used to call their 'little demons.' One single word, one single big, fat, well-planted calendar chromo, the minute it's dropped in there, is like a particle of crystal dropped into a supersaturated liquid: suddenly everything is petrified, everything hardens. They grow a shell. They become inert and heavy. . . . I can see them—the old man too, despite his air of disillusionment, his air of one who, "having understood all, has forgiven all," which he always assumes, he is exactly like her, they resemble each other—I can see the scene between them, I can see their encounter, see them with their foreheads pressed together in close combat, hunched up in their shells, in their heavy armor: "I am the Father, the Daughter, my Rights." They are enclosed in it. They can't break away. . . . The blind, relentless struggle of two giant insects, two enormous dung beetles. . . ."

But he still looked somewhat displeased. He seemed to be ill at ease, embarrassed. He laid his hand on my arm: "Curiously enough, I was thinking about you just the other day: I met him, the old man, as you call him, and he put on a little act for me which would have interested you. . . . As usual, in his rough, funny way . . . the way he flings words about like lassoes. . . . You know. . . . With his habitual hearty laughter. . . . 'Well, how is everything? Eh? What's up? Time marches on? We change, eh? We're growing older. . . . And how's everybody? How are the children? We change . . . we get into another category . . . we change categories. You know what I mean, don't you, by categories? You know what I mean? Son, father, grandfather categories, mother, daughter categories . . . ?' He began to laugh his queer laughter, which is always somewhat hollow; he kept on: 'Eh, eh, categories? Father . . . daughter. . . .' I had the feeling that he had taken me by the scruff of the neck and was rubbing my nose in it, like someone training a puppy. I could feel that he was trying to 'get me.' I can tell you one thing, however; he's not taken in, he doesn't believe in it himself. If I were you, I should be on my guard." He looked straight ahead, smiling to himself with a gently secret smile, almost of affection: "And as for her, do you remember what sensitive taste she used to have, the rather astonishing things she scribbled in the margin of the *Illuminations?* You remember her expression, when she sensed something a bit dubious (she had an unerring instinct), the expression: 'It's warmed over. . . . It's a cliché. . . .'" He sent a rapid glance in my direction: "An expression you both used. . . . She said it with a sneer, with her gutter accent, half caustic, half affected . . . it's . . . a . . . cli-i-ché . . . with the slurred vowels wallowing in the back of her throat. It used to make you sick. . . . You hated her so. . . ." He thought a moment: "It's curious, really, that it should also be an expression you like . . . one of your expressions. . . ." We grew silent. I sensed that he was afraid he had wounded me way down somewhere, in a particularly sensitive spot. He tried to turn back. He would have liked to make me a slight compensation: "However, in reality, I don't know . . . you may be right . . . you are certainly right, in any case, as regards a whole category of people. . . . Like my mother for instance, or my aunt . . . the 'demanding' kind . . . for them, I don't deny it . . . your little idea applies very well to them. . . . By the way, the other day. . . ." I sensed that he was slipping awkwardly into anecdotes, gossip (the thing I detest most), but I nevertheless made an effort to appear interested, I asked him questions, even took my turn at telling stories: under no circumstances should the torpid, agreeable water in which we were immersed—the luke-warm bath of our intimacy—be allowed to cool off.

We stayed there for a long time, becoming more and more soft and weakened as a result of endless soaking, endless going over and over the same things. . . . The room was nearly empty. The smoke hurt my eyes. I felt a vague uneasiness, like a slight nausea—a sort of annoyance as when one has been eating peanuts or sunflower seeds for a long time and can't stop, or when one bites one's nails. I had the impression of chewing on air. I should have liked to get up and leave, but I couldn't bring myself to face the wrench, the cold, painful embarrassment that seizes upon us each time we are about to separate, after one of our little pleasure parties.

I knew it perfectly, I had known it perfectly well already, deep down inside, during the time when I was hurrying, filled with joy and hope, towards the café. I knew that I should do better to go home, bury myself in my own corner and examine all alone, without showing it to anybody, the discovery I had made, make still another effort, to go into it more deeply, all by myself. But it's beyond me: I can't resist a certain need I have, as soon as I notice the slightest semblance of success on the horizon, to postpone the ultimate effort, to relax right away, to play around, endlessly relishing the anticipation; above all, however, I can't resist the need to cheapen myself. That has been my ruin, I know it. . . . Look at it now, that great discovery, that little "vision" of mine, look what had become of it, after we had once more subjected it to our pernicious children's games, our catlike games: there it lay between us, torn in shreds, gray and motionless, a dead mouse.

"Whom are you slandering now?" This cut through me all of a sudden. It pierced me and riveted me to the bench.

(Even now I have only to recall it to, as they say, "blush to the roots of my hair." I get all hot.)

"Whom are you slandering now?" She had come nearer to us, having slipped between the tables without our seeing her, we were once more so absorbed, our heads together, talking, very excitedly, deep in our favorite games. "Whom are you slandering now?" We started with just a few mild jerks, like galvanized frogs, before we turned to stone, riveted to our seats, weak, frozen smiles on our faces. It was a clever stroke. One of those skillful, sure strokes such as they know how to give, similar to the marvelously accurate javelin strokes with which certain insects are said to paralyze their enemies by striking straight into the nerve centers. Once the first moment of amazement had passed, and we had come to ourselves again, I felt my friend looking at me with admiration, as he sometimes does (ho! ho! not bad, that . . .) he always attributes visitations of this kind to me, it seems to him, as it does to me, that it is I who call them forth, I who provoke them.

She sat down at our table: "I'm not disturbing you?" This time she was sure of herself, entirely offhanded. I realized that it was his presence that made her that way. There is something elusive about him which they all feel immediately, something that holds them in check and keeps them from brimming over: he acts on them like a plaster cast on bones that are too soft or twisted, he holds them in place, sets them straight; just the opposite of myself who always have the same kind of mysterious influence on them that the moon has on the tides: I always stir up currents and ground swells and eddies in them; with me they expand, grow excited and brim over, I unleash them;

he, on the contrary, probably without intending to do so —these things are always unconscious—holds them in leash. In any case, we neutralized each other, he and I, and he even won out: she appeared to be in complete control of herself, very calm. She seemed to ignore me. They had begun to talk between themselves about the book she was carrying (I believe it was something or other like *Stèles*, by Ségalen). I realized that in this state of salutary listlessness to which he had reduced her, she hardly took me into account, she treated me as though I were entirely negligible; I realized, too, that, as always when she is in that state, she considered me as a somewhat childish, unpolished, uncultivated person. I felt that right away by the slightly negligent manner with which she listened to the few remarks I had splutteringly attempted to inject into their conversation, before she turned away from me. I am so easily influenced, I too am so sensitive to suggestion. The impression people have of me rubs off on me right away, I become exactly the way they see me, right away and in spite of myself.

However, I did my best, as soon as I could, to add my grain of salt to their conversation, but without the slightest success, in a timid, unsteady voice, the one I always have as soon as I feel unsure of myself. I kept thinking about the tormenting need I feel, like an itch, as soon as I see her, to make up to her, my need to appease and charm her.

As we were about to say good-bye, while she was shaking my hand outside, on the sidewalk, I saw once more, for a brief, very rapid moment, the hunted look in her eyes:

51

she was in a hurry to leave us now, she was afraid, undoubtedly, to be alone with me.

Only, this time, I wouldn't let myself be taken in: "So you are going that way? It just happens, that is the direction I was going, I can go that way, too. . . . No, not at all, that doesn't make it any longer. . . ." She would have liked to get out of it, but there was no way to do so; I attached myself to her, I followed her. . . . At the corner we both crossed the street and together we stepped onto the pavement and started down the Boulevard du Port Royal. . . . I clung to her like her shadow. . . . "Little jaunts of this type," she would say, "are distinctly warmed-over stuff. A device. Somewhat in the manner of Dostoievsky. Vaguely reminiscent of slightly similar scenes in *The Eternal Husband* or *The Idiot* . . . pure literature. . . ." I knew, . . . I knew well, that it was infinitely more likely that, after having shaken hands with her, I should have gone home. I knew that that's what should have happened, it should have been my turn to "run," somewhat bent over, leaning a bit forward the better to support, the better to bear, until I reached home, this burden, this oppressive suffering within myself; I should have hidden in my corner like a sick dog. Only I've had enough. No more of that. Enough. I've been "taken in" enough by them. They have made game of me long enough. I won't stand for it any more. I won't give in. I don't give in. . . . We walked on, side by side. By now we were walking along the wall on the Boulevard du Port Royal: the long, dreary wall of an almshouse or a hospital, one of those walls that Rilke came across at every turn during the melancholy strolls of his early visits to Paris. It is against the background of this wall that I always see the cab in which the livid face of the man with the bandage lolled above his gauze-swathed neck. Today there is nothing that so readily creates about a wall a sort of tragic, scenic, almost hallucinatory atmosphere, as to project against it the black, unreal, poignant form of a cab.

This wall suited me quite well as a background. Our dark silhouettes stood out against it: she, with her flattened-out back and her thin legs striding along, her head stretched out in front like a fist, her bulging, hard eyes staring straight ahead of her; I, trotting along beside her, looking at her sidewise, wearing the strange, obsequious, sinister, inane, exasperating smile that used to appear at similar moments on the face of the Eternal Husband. But watch out. I've stopped playing. Here we are. Watch out. All bets are off. *Les jeux sont faits.* Now we've stopped, facing each other, on the corner of the Rue Berthollet. She looks at me. Her eyes stop moving. They are riveted on me. Two large, hard marbles pressing against my eyes: a vestige of the self-assurance she had shown before. Or else she feels what is coming and is pressing against me with all her force in order to push me away, to hold me back. But she won't stop me.

There are certain words—as innocuous in appearance as passwords—which I never pronounce before her, I am careful not to do so. I always skirt around them from afar, I take precautions to avoid them, when she is there I continue to watch all approaches, in order to keep them from turning up, and if anyone, through ignorance or innocence, pronounces them in her presence before me, I pretend, in order to put her at her ease, to have seen nothing, I assume the unconscious, absent-minded manner that tactful or easily embarrassed persons affect in a sickroom when the commode or the enema bag is brought in.

These words frighten me considerably. If I were to say them before her, it should be like pulling the dressing off an open wound. . . . "Flayed alive. . . ." "Hypersensitive. . . ." It seems to me I would be uncovering her wounds.

But this time I've made up my mind, I am as calm as a surgeon beside the operating table, as he pulls on his gloves and picks up his forceps: delicately I take hold of a corner of the dressing . . . I begin to pull: "And what about your father? How is he? I heard you had moved? Don't you live with him any more?" Her eyes shift from side to side as though seeking a way of escape, a muscle in her cheek begins to twitch, her face is contracted and tense, as though it were about to crack, she says nothing—she probably is unable to speak—taking all my courage in hand, I continue to pull; off comes the whole thing: articulating each word (I'm so frightened that I have the impression that I'm shouting, my voice resounds on the entire boulevard), I say: "That must be hard for you. The family. You can say what you want. One's father. That's something nothing can take the place of. A father is a sanctuary, a haven, a port of refuge from the storms of Life. The most dependable mainstay of all. . . ." I watch her. Just as in fairy tales, as soon as the magic incantation is spoken, the charm begins to work, the metamorphosis takes place, all her features appear to sag, I have the impression that they are falling apart, stretching and trembling as though reflected in water or in a distorting mirror, and then her face becomes absolutely flat, her head slumps into her shoulders and leans slightly in my direction as though asking for alms, her eyes fill with tears, she sniffles and wipes her nose, like a child, with the back of her hand: "Oh! do you think so? You believe that too? You know, he's not easy. He can't understand. . . . Sometimes. . . . I can tell you it's not easy for a woman alone. And I have no one else. . . ."

To see her prone like that, sprawling there before me, acquiescent, made me want to take her by her taut neck and hurl her over the housetops, I should have liked to see her flying over the chimney stacks, emitting piercing shrieks, pedaling the air with her crooked legs, her black cape flying in the breeze, like the witches in fairy tales. Unfortunately, however, we were not in a fairy tale. I had to curb the feeling of disgust and hatred that came over me. Keep calm. Hang on.

At present my *alter* could tell me as often as he pleased to watch out—she's so subtle, so shrewd, she has undoubtedly understood my game, and is perhaps playing one of her own in order to make fun of me and see how far I will go—I wouldn't believe him. There's no danger of that. I have spoken the words that, in her case, put an immediate end to all joking, to all sneers and attitudes of cynicism and disgust; I have spoken the words that make her bow her head religiously the way the sound of the altar bell bows the heads of the faithful. I have opened the portals of the Sacred Domain, into which she enters only with the deepest respect, even fear, and in which she would never—oh! no, not in that domain, that would be too indecorous, too much of a risk—indulge in scoffing. . . . We have entered the Sacred Domain of "Life," as they call it, of "Realities," of "harsh Necessity," as they say with a sigh, nodding assent, with an air of resignation: "That's how life is, the harsh realities of life. . . ." Just here she always hesitates, she's afraid, she doesn't know, she has so little confidence in herself, she is so lacking in assurance, she needs people's approval, and guidance. . . . Oh! she's very modest, doesn't go in for niceties, not at all pretentious, not at all, not when it is a matter of that . . . distinctions, or the refinements of life, that's all right for other people, you understand, she can't afford them, they're beyond her means. What she tries for, is to avoid especially anything that might shock people, or appear to be abnormal and out of place, all pretentiousness or eccentricity; she is perfectly satisfied with well-tried, substantial, inexpensive things; ready-made, good standardized merchandise suits her perfectly, and even, I've noticed this, she rather has a preference, which might appear almost perverse to anyone who knows her, for the cheapest kind of trash, the shoddiest kind of dimestore stuff.

In the same way that the white-collar worker or the little coupon clipper, when he is choosing his dining room or bedroom "suite," inquires, at once anxiously and a bit shamefacedly, of the salesman—so little has he confidence in his own taste, he feels so helpless and doesn't dare rely on his own impressions, or show his own preferences—whether the picture he wants to buy to hang over the mantelpiece is "good," will "go well" with the rest, with this particular furniture, whether it will harmonize with the wallpaper and the color of the curtains, she too goes around with a submissive, silly, dull expression, asking—she doesn't know, she must be advised, encouraged, she is so afraid of making a mistake, she doesn't dare rely on herself—she keeps asking: "Oh! yes, you really think I'm right, that it's natural and normal for me to suffer this way, for me to miss him as I do, for me, still, even at my age, to have such need of him . . . ? You do think so? Really . . . ? Because, you know, he can't understand that. . . ."

It is in order to hear what they will say, to win them over, and obtain their support, that she stands before them, the way I see her standing before me now, her hands folded modestly like the hands of old women with faded, washed-out faces; it is doubtless in order to obtain their entire approval, to prove to them that she is one of their own—the slightest critical glance, the slightest shrinking back on their part would frighten her so—that she has gotten herself up like this. I look her over: she is entirely in black with bits of crepe, certainly mourning worn for an aunt or a grandmother; she has donned those gray cotton gloves and coarse black cotton stockings that give her legs a mottled look; it is in order the better to be identified with them, to show her submissiveness, to attract no attention . . . like the accent she affects, too, a feeble, mincing accent, with cringing vowel sounds. When she is with them there is never the slightest caustic or aggressive note about her accent.

With the result that they are always taken in, they're never on their guard. The women who meet on their door-steps, or in the stairway, carrying their market bags, look at her in a friendly way. Nothing dubious, nothing improper or vaguely disturbing about her prompts them to be on their guard. She doesn't have to prick up her ears, on the floor below, waiting, with beating heart, to hear their infallible judgment, their verdict. She doesn't have to listen at keyholes or be content with the crumbs from their table.

Their placid, kindly faces smile at her, they bend and sway gently, marking their approval, their pity: "If that isn't a shame. . . . A man of his age, and so unreasonable. . . . And when I think that you are all he has in the world, and what's it for? What good is it to him? He can't take it with him, that's certain. You might understand . . ." they go on, because they always like to reason from an ever higher vantage point, only progressing very slowly, in order to first make sure of their conquered territory, before advancing new arguments . . . "You might understand if he were a poor man, or if he had other children, you have to think of everything of course . . . or say he had remarried, sometimes these young women can change a man entirely. . . . It was like that, you know, with poor Mr. Dufaux, nobody recognized him after his second marriage, he let his son starve to death, literally refused to see him. . . . Still he was lucky enough, poor boy, to get a job in his uncle's garage. . . . And yet they had plenty, I can tell you, plenty of money and plenty of property, if only counting the 'Old Mill,' for instance, which he got from his first wife, and what a lot of money they sank into it. . . ." She doesn't grow impatient, but waits respectfully, not daring to hurry them, for the long, viscous links of their arguments to unwind before her, and she nods approval, *ee-y-ess,* in a rapt, interested fashion, she hardly dares even to set them right when they stray a bit too far afield, or lose sight of their goal: "Oh! yes, of course, I understand, but you see in my case, it's not at all the same thing, I'm all he has left in the world you know, since my poor mother died. . . ." They shake their heads: "The fact is, he's a real egoist, men like that shouldn't have the right to bring children into the

58

world. And when you think how many people there are who'd give anything to have their daughter with them in their old age to take care of them. But you'd be making a great mistake if you let him get the upper hand. There are lots of people, that I can tell you, who haven't got your tact and who would make no bones about it, they just simply wouldn't have agreed to live apart from him. After all, no matter what he does, you'll always be his daughter and he'll always be your father. You can't get around that, now can you?"

She drinks in avidly their heavy, leaden words which flow down into her very depths and ballast her. Inert and ponderous, she commits herself into their hands—a lifeless object which they are going to push, which they are going to hurl at him, which will move towards him with the precise, blind, unrelenting movement of a torpedo following the path of its trajectory. Nothing will stop her, nothing will make her deviate from her course.

A mask—that is the word I always use, although it is not exactly suitable, to describe the expression he assumes as soon as she comes in, or even before she comes in, when he has heard nothing but the faint scratch of her key in the lock, or her quick, dry little ring, or the sound of her lowered, very soft voice in the hall, or simply when he feels her approach—he has such sensitive antennae—her silent presence on the other side of the wall. Immediately, as though actuated by some sort of automatic trigger, his face changes: it grows heavy and taut, taking on the very special, artificial, stiff expression that people often have when they look at themselves in the mirror, or else that strange, rather hard-to-define aspect that we sometimes see on the faces of people who have submitted to plastic surgery.

It is more than probable—and for my part I am certain of it—that this is the expression he must always have worn in her presence. It is surely the very expression that he had worn at the moment of their first contact, when she was still but a child in her cradle; at the moment, doubtless, when he heard for the first time her stubborn, strident cry; or perhaps, even at the moment when, as he leaned over the cradle the better to see her, he felt the downy, aggressive outline of her overwide nostrils, distended upwards as she cried, pierce through him and pain him, the way the silken edge of certain sharp grasses cuts insidiously into the flesh.

Certain very sensitive persons, such as he, feel their face tauten and draw like that even with very young children. They need next to nothing, they are so frail, so responsive to the slightest breath, like a delicate pendulum that trembles and starts to swing under the influence of even a very weak current.

I have known several who had never been able to assume any other expression, even in the presence of their own child (shall we say, especially in its presence), and that was when the child was still quite young and innocent.

Innocent, doubtless, in appearance only. Because they're never entirely innocent, are they, never entirely above suspicion: something intangible emanates from them, a tenuous, clinging thread, delicate little suckers like those that stretch, trembling, on the end of the hairs that line carnivorous plants; or else, a sticky juice like the silk

62

secreted by silkworms: something indefinable and mysterious, that adheres to the other person's face and pulls it, or else spreads over it like a gluey coating, under which it petrifies.

Some of these unfortunate creatures, perhaps vaguely conscious that something oozes from them, themselves assume an inscrutable, rigid expression, with all exits blocked, as though to keep these mysterious effluvia from escaping; or perhaps it is in a spirit of imitation, the result of suggestion—they are so easily influenced, so sensitive—that they, too, in the presence of the masks, take on that set, dead expression. Others, in spite of themselves, dance about like puppets, twitching nervously and making faces. Still others, in order to get into the good graces of the mask and restore life to its stony features, play the clown and stoop to any lengths to provoke laughter at their own expense. Others, even more contemptibly—these are generally the older, more vicious ones—as a result of a sort of irresistible attraction, sidle up like a dog rubbing against its master's leg, beg for a pat or an affectionate gesture that will calm their fears, and lie wriggling on their backs, all four feet in the air: they chatter away, open wide their hearts, grow confidential and, in a voice that lacks assurance, blushingly tell their most intimate secrets to the motionless mask.

But the mask won't give in. It simply won't let itself be taken in. On the contrary, all these contortions and flummery more often than not only serve to make it grow harder.

It would be difficult to say exactly whether it is in spite of itself, and without knowing very well why, that the mask keeps growing harder like this, or whether it doesn't deliberately overact, in order to punish the person who has stooped to these degrading buffooneries in its presence, and so increase the smart of baseness; whether it is in order to discourage the opponent, by playing dead like a fox at the approach of an enemy, to defend itself against these contacts and these repulsive wrigglings; or whether, on the contrary, it is in the unconscious desire to foment these goings-on in order to make the game more exciting, and thus prolong and relish for a greater length of time a subtle kind of secret, sensual pleasure.

I have no idea. Nobody has any idea. Nobody has ever given it a thought. They've all got other fish to fry, other, more worth-while, more legitimate things to think about. Even those who appear to have touched upon this question have never condescended to pause over it for a while.

As it happens, there is a character in a novel about whom the masks always make me think, and that is the very "well-drawn," "vivid" character of the hero in *War and Peace,* old Prince Bolkonski. I used to know him well in the old days, he was a friend of my youth—in fact, it was this very same mask, I am certain of it, that he must have worn in the presence of his daughter, Princess Marie. But Tolstoy doesn't say so, or rather he barely hints at it, in passing.

And yet I am ready to make a bet that it is this same mask that she always saw him wear: at table, where he presided, an imposing figure, under his powdered wig; in the morning, when she went, trembling, into his study, and he held out his rough cheek for her to kiss; or else, when she came across him on one of the paths on the estate, making his tour of inspection, followed by his overseer.

There was only one time, one single time, at the very last moment, when he was about to die, that as she leaned over him to try to catch the words he was stammering with the greatest effort because of his paralyzed tongue—perhaps it was *douchenka,* my little soul, or *droujok,* my little friend, she couldn't catch it, it was so extraordinary, so unexpected—only at that moment did she see the mask relax for the first time. It broke down and became another face, a new face she had never seen before, pitiful, a bit childish even, shy and tender.

That must have been, I believe, either the day of, or the day before, his death.

There is every reason to believe (and Tolstoy, no doubt, also thought so) that he had always held himself stiff and contracted, lest something in him that was too powerful and too violent break through and overspread everything: a feeling, a love, perhaps, so violent that he had the impression it could escape from him like a mad bull, or a howling, hungry wolf, and which he held fast under his hard, inscrutable mask.

At times, when he was unable to hold it in any longer, he would let it explode briefly in the most distorted forms: hideous contortions, sneering laughter, shouts and bitter tongue lashings.

It was not until the very last moment—there was nothing more to be afraid of: death was near and his strength gone—that he dared to unscrew the valve that compressed it, and his love, benumbed and unsure of gait, escaped from him.

How, indeed, could it have been anything else? One had only to look at Princess Marie, who seemed all innocence and purity. There was nothing dubious, apparently, about her; no affectation, no ignoble quiverings, never any shameful attempts to run away from the inevitable, or to fly in the face of fact. She accepted her fate with a resignation that was filled with dignity.

And yet, like the tramp in I forget which play, who kept repeating, as he shook his head incredulously, while one of his fellow tramps described in glowing colors the marvelous, much-to-be-envied lives of the rich: "I'd have to see for myself," I, too, am inclined to say that I'd like to "see" for myself. The case of Princess Marie was, probably, not so simple as that. There must be some slight, barely suggested indications—we should have to look for them, I believe, in her rather timorous nature, or in her shyness, or else in her great refinement (all three of which are to be mistrusted)—there are certain indications which make me think that this great love of Prince Bolkonski's (if, indeed, we may use the word love in describing his feeling: as always, it is impossible to escape these big words that bowl us right over), this love of his was probably to be found in a situation somewhat like that of Gulliver, as he lay bound by the thousand ties of the Lilliputians, his body riddled with their tiny arrows.

A thousand extremely fine and hardly discernible threads —here we have again the trembling, sticky threads of the Virgin—must have gone forth continually from Princess Marie to cling to him and, eventually, cover him over.

Death alone was able to do what no amount of effort on their part could have accomplished: with one sweep it cleared away those thousand tenuous feelings that constituted the daily warp and woof of their life, abruptly it severed all these ties: the cocoon opened and "love" emerged awkwardly, fluttering for a second like a delicate butterfly, its wings still crumpled: *douchenka,* my little soul—it was hard to catch what he was saying—or, perhaps, *droujok,* my little friend.

But I realize that all this is the merest, rather rough supposition, so much daydreaming.

Far cleverer men than I might break both tooth and nail in some such insolent attempt to grapple with Prince Bolkonski, or with Princess Marie.

For it should not be forgotten that they are really somebody. They belong among those characters in fiction who are so successfully portrayed that we are accustomed to refer to them as "real," or "alive," more real and more alive, in fact, than the living themselves.

The memories we retain of persons we have known are no sharper, no more "alive" than the precise little colored images engraved in our minds by, shall we say, the soft Russian leather boot, embroidered in silver, that the old prince wore; or his fur-lined velvet jacket with the sable collar and cap, or his bony, hard hands that clutched like pincers, his dry little old man's hands with their prominent veins, and the continual scenes he made, and his tongue lashings. Often these things seem to us to be more "real," more "true," than all the similar scenes we ourselves ever took part in.

In that vast museum in which we preserve the people we have known and loved, and to which we refer, no doubt, when we speak of our "knowledge of life," these characters occupy a privileged position.

And, like the people we know best, even those nearest to us, among whom we ourselves live, each one of them appears to us as a finished, perfect whole, entirely enclosed on every side, a solid, hard block, without a single fissure, a smooth sphere that offers nothing the hand can grasp. Their actions, which maintain them in a state of perpetual motion, shape, isolate and protect them, hold them in a standing position, that is, erect and impregnable, the way a waterspout is formed, sucked up and erected so solidly by the violent force of the wind outside the ocean, that even a cannon ball is unable to destroy it.

How I should like to see all the misshapen tatters, the trembling shadows, the ghosts, the ghouls and the larvae that flout me and which I nevertheless pursue—take on those same smooth, well-rounded forms, present those same pure, firm outlines.

How delightful and peaceful it would be to see them become part of the cheerful circle of familiar faces.

But for this to happen, I realize perfectly, I should have to bring myself to accept certain risks, to launch out a bit, to begin with, if only on a single point, no matter which one, it's of no importance. As, for instance, to give them at least a name to identify them with. That would already be a first step towards isolating them, towards rounding them off a little and giving them a certain consistency. That would serve to establish them somewhat. But I just can't do it. There's no use pretending. I know it would be just so much pain for nothing. . . . It wouldn't take people long to find out what kind of merchandise I was transporting under this flag. My own. The only kind I have to offer.

Rich ornaments, warm colors, soothing certainties, the fresh sweetness of "life," are not for me. When, occasionally, these "live" persons, or these characters, condescend to come near me too, all I am able to do is to hover about them and try with fanatical eagerness to find the crack, the tiny crevice, the weak point, as delicate as a baby's fontanelle, at which I seem to see something that resembles a barely perceptible pulsation suddenly swell and begin to throb gently. I cling to it and press upon it. And then I feel a strange substance trickling from them in an endless stream, a substance as anonymous as lymph, or blood, an insipid liquid that flows through my hands and spills. . . . And all that remains of the firm, rosy, velvety flesh of these "live" persons is a shapeless gray covering, from which all blood has been drained away.

I've given up. I've handed myself over bound hand and foot. The masks have been my undoing. Once more, everything came out, just when I thought I had succeeded in holding it in. Now I'm back in line. I had to do it. You can't live with impunity among larvae. The game becomes unhealthy. In fact, people around me were beginning to express alarm. I decided to make the first move. Only this time, not by sidling up to them insidiously to plead with them—I know that doesn't work, they only brush me off—but by coming out in the open, by complete submission: let them do what they want with me, if only they will release me, I can't go on, I've given up, I withdraw entirely.

In such cases as mine, the stubborn cases that have failed to react to ordinary raps, or to the idle gaze of someone who is not interested in these things, they resort to specialists. It doesn't take these chaps long to get the upper hand of all the so-called different "visions" that are outside the realm of "artistic research," as well as entirely useless, and may occasionally, when they become chronic, bring on rather serious disturbances. They straighten all that out in no time and pigeonhole it in their own way. That private little idea, or that private little vision of yours that you had been brooding over with mingled pride and shyness, is labeled and tossed in among others in the same category. In fact, they're all alike, apparently, when examined closely: "These unhappy persons keep going round and round in a rather narrow circle"—that's probably the way they talk —"although their musings may assume countless apparently diverse forms." Specialists know how to set all that straight.

I must say for mine, the one I went to, it was I myself who put him on the right track. Just the little trick of refusing to mention names, the way I like to say "they," as soon as I did that in front of him, he saw it right away. It's a rather characteristic sign, apparently. This didn't surprise me, in fact I had always suspected it. I saw that he was observing me, without seeming to do so—they are very clever and tactful—that he was watching for another symptom, which would have been very helpful, too, in the matter of classification: doubtless that sort of secret pride, that is so well known, and always crops out in the end—like a running wound. But on this point, I imagine he must have been disappointed. As I said before, I don't try to be different. I ask nothing better than to be rid of it all and find release. I explained to him carefully that it was this, especially, which had made me agree to see him. He surely must understand that: these throbbings and shudderings, these reaching tentacles and larvae, were, after all, in his department. I asked nothing better than to spread it all out before him. I mentioned "them." He smiled—very politely, however—a fleeting, somewhat patronizing, tolerant smile. No matter. I didn't take exception to it. It was already a great relief to know that he understood what it was all about and to see that he was prepared to listen to me patiently and calmly, without brushing me off. Also, with him, I felt nothing of the rather painful promiscuity which I sometimes felt with my *alter*.

I told him everything, just as it came, the best I could, especially the "scenes" between them, that moment when they confront each other, that attracts me and which I fall into like a dark hole; the way they have, too, of springing up from nowhere, and the painful fascination they always exert upon me. He finds this normal: "That's a very usual thing," he says, "nervous people, sensitive as they are to what you call 'effluvia' or 'currents,' always seek out one another. These people of yours are highly nervous individuals. To be convinced of this fact, one has only to consider the predominant role played, in their case, by 'scenes.' And also by the clichés you describe and which, as you say, they affect in order to confront each other, to legitimize their clashes. This is a frequent feature of the neuropath; his submission to the cliché, which you have identified very accurately, in fact, but which, in my opinion, has nothing disquieting or mysterious about it. Don't take offense"—

he's very intelligent, he's found it right away, the hiding place of that little secret pride, he never makes a mistake: in the presence of all the other symptoms, he knows that he has only to hunt, and the missing symptom will always turn up—"don't take it to heart, many a literary character who has since become famous, was, from our point of view, a neurotic. But it looks to me as though, in the case that seems to be plaguing you, everything is apparently very simple. In this connection, you might read quietly at home my article treating of these types of conformity, types that are very frequent among nervous people." I have the impression that he thinks it is time to end the interview: other patients are waiting in the reception room. As for that, the consultation has already given results. Already, little by little, I am beginning to be "in contact with reality" —supposedly a symptom of recovery. I feel it by the way "they" have changed in appearance. They have come nearer and are growing hard and finished, with clear colors and distinct outlines, only rather like the painted cardboard dolls that serve as targets in street fairs. One more click of the trigger and down they'll fall.

Before rising to leave, I attempt to make a clean breast of everything. But I feel that he is growing a little bit impatient, really he hasn't the time, it would require a number of long, costly consultations—for that matter, if I felt the need to do so, one of his pupils could very well undertake it—to dissect my "visions" in detail. But somehow I keep on talking to him, falteringly, about masks, and then—but this is more out of a desire to clear my conscience, because I know what he's going to say—I make so bold as to bring up the subject of Prince Bolkonski. I feel myself redden a bit. He is smiling slightly: "Of course, I am not an art critic, and I would not undertake to express definitive opinions in these matters. It seems to me, however, that the role of all creative effort in the arts is, precisely, to clothe abstraction. Look at Bergson." He gives me a slightly mocking glance: "Show us a person who is really alive and, if it gives you any pleasure, put any kind of mask you want on him. But make him live first, make him concrete, tangible. Try and get away from all these sterile musings, these ideas that remain in the stage of inconsistent, naked ideas: neither fish nor fowl, neither science nor material for artistic creation. And above all, watch out, all that goes together" (he rises and holds out his hand, quite evidently the interview has lasted too long), "watch out for your tendency towards introspection and idle daydreaming, which is nothing other than evasion of effort. Then, believe me, you will see for yourself that there are few 'phantoms,' few 'ghosts' in life, worthy of the name."

When the three of us reached the street, I and my aging parents, who had taken me to him, I saw that they were a bit disconcerted, not to say, embarrassed; in fact, they seemed to be slightly humiliated; it was as though they had grown more shriveled, more shrunken than usual. And yet, at the same time, I knew that they felt a certain satisfaction, without realizing it, perhaps. Their limp, old hands, with their overred palms and brittle nails, yellow and lined, patted my arm affectionately, the way they used to do when the three of us went walking on Sunday. Our footsteps echoed loudly along the hot, deserted street, as they had done on those far-off summer Sundays. I felt weak and a bit unsteady, the way one feels when one goes out for the first time after a long illness. As I walked slowly along beside them, adapting my pace to theirs, I had that same sense of slight nausea and dizziness that one feels in an elevator when it leaves the floor level and sinks gently down into the void.

Crossing the square where I had once made mudpies at their feet, they led me to the cake shop we had always patronized. At the sight of the cakes and the friendly, bright smile of the salesgirl, their humble manner almost disappeared, they seemed to perk up a bit, and as they plied me with chocolate éclairs, they began to question me, setting me insidiously on the right path, with hardly perceptible little taps on the back, following the advice of the specialist, no doubt, to give me "a sense of reality" or rather, as I realized perfectly, they were simply letting themselves go, now that I no longer had the force to make them keep their distance: they asked about certain of my schoolmates, people we used to know, whatever became of Paul? And what news of Jeanne? They say her marriage is a failure. . . . Was it true that she had gone to work in order to help her old mother? And what about Germaine's husband? It seems they've bought a very nice country place and their son is studying at Polytechnique? Already. . . . Shaking their heads, they gave a sigh of satisfied resignation: "Heavens, how time does fly. . . ." I agreed, and continued to tell them stories, forced to lean down towards them, lower and still lower (bite the dust, I said to myself, but I hadn't the strength to resist, I would have to give in now, I had nothing left, nothing that was my own, nothing to keep back from them, nothing I could withhold from their reach); to please them, I made their puppets dance for them, I accompanied them slowly through their museum, took part in the review of their tin soldiers. . . .

Content and confident, now they were smiling. Their avid, flabby hands continued to stroke me affectionately, as though to encourage me. I let them do it. I felt myself growing weaker and weaker, drained dry, and then I was afraid to break away from them abruptly. I even stuck to them more and more, I clung to them, I was beginning already to feel something rising up inside me, something throbbing gently in a void, rising, falling, the way an imperfectly closed shutter knocks in the silence of the night—I stuck to them, because I knew that if I were suddenly to be left alone, without them, in the hot deserted street, the throbbing would echo inside me with a frightful noise.

Ambivalence; that was something to have discovered—the sort of mingled revulsion and attraction, a coexistence in the same individual, with respect to the same object, of love and hatred. A few poets, a few very clever writers, succeeded a long time ago in digging this up and bringing it out into the light, but without giving it a name. The specialists, however, have successfully identified it. Mine had explained it to me very carefully. He was very suspicious (he had had wide experience with these cases) with regard to the sincerity of my resolution to return to the straight and narrow path: "The trouble with people like you," he had told me, "is that they lie to themselves. Their desire to get well is more often than not accompanied by no less great a reluctance to give up the advantages and satisfactions they derive from their illness—alas, this has to be said, however real their suffering, which I don't deny."

And yet it seemed to me that I was really acting in good faith. There were still moments when I would discover in myself a tinge of rancorous regret, as when I took a sort of bitter pleasure in repeating (the last gasps of pride, no doubt) the following words which come back to me now and then from heaven knows where, and which, in my bad moments, I like to apply to myself: "They ate off my plate. . . . They spat in my bowl . . . desecrated my food . . . sullied the water in my spring. . . ."

But these moments were rare. Most of the time I really couldn't discover in myself the slightest desire to revert to my former tormented states. I had become docility itself. Little by little, I had grown accustomed to going quietly about my business, like all those around me who lived in their calm, serene world of distinctly drawn outlines, as different from the viscous, gloomy world in which they, he and she, plagued me, as is the adult world from that of the muffled, indistinctly outlined world of childhood. I was exorcised. Like the lover who, at one time, used to feel his heart leap and his hand tremble at the mere sight on an unknown face of the tilt of an eyebrow or the curve of a cheek that vaguely recalled the face of his beloved, and who realizes to his astonishment, when he no longer loves her, that none of her features or expressions, none of the little mannerisms which used to seem so moving and mysterious to him has any further meaning for him, and that he is unable to recapture in them any trace of the strange vibration which once transmitted itself to him and made him tremble so violently, I would occasionally feel now a certain astonishment that they should strike me, he and she, as being so innocuous, a matter of indifference to which I attached no interest, no importance. Now, on turning a corner or crossing a public square, I could see the meek line of their backs without experiencing any of the swooning sensations I used to feel.

So I was able to go away with a clear conscience and with general approval. In such cases as mine, a voyage is always advisable, and my family let me leave without the slightest opposition. They probably knew that they now had me well in hand and that I would not break loose from myself again: they could hold the leash a little less tightly; or perhaps I had already progressed to the point of having acquired the rather special quiet, dignified docility characteristic of strong people, and which commands respect.

The specialist, in fact, had greatly encouraged me. He was very much in favor of this voyage as a practical means of combating introversion: "Forget all that," he had told me, "quit mulling over it, and live your life as it comes. Model yourself—I realize that you will probably consider this 'character' as a bit out of date," here he had given me one of his embarrassed, slightly mocking smiles—"model yourself on Nathanaël, and partake of the 'terrestrial viands'—try to recapture a sense of 'fervor'—that is what you need now to complete your cure."

Nevertheless, it was already at this point that ambivalence must have come into play. Surreptitiously, as usual, and without my knowing it: in the very choice of a city.

And yet this city seemed to me to present no complications whatsoever. On the contrary, it seemed to guarantee success. For me it was, and had always been, the city of the *Invitation au Voyage*. It's almost imperceptibly rocking boats (Baudelaire had also considered the word 'waddling,' he had hesitated, but in the end had found a way of saying it still better), the masts of vessels lying in the old harbor, the sky, the waters, the canals, were all suffused with a sort of rhapsodical softness. The words of the *Invitation au Voyage* struck it lightly and it began to vibrate with melodious sound, as pure and transparent and clear as crystal. One had only to pronounce the words softly: *"les soleils couchants revêtent les champs, les canaux, la ville entière d'hyacinthe et d'or,"* and at the words: *"la ville entière,"* it rose up in a single impulse, its main street opened out like an oriflamme, hung with flags and banners, waving in the soft sea breeze, through the golden light.

This was purified, decanted matter, fine matter, well wrought. An exquisite dish, ready to eat. One had only to serve oneself. And, indeed, my anticipation was not disappointed. In fact, my condition being so close to recovery helped considerably: I had grown more flexible, more receptive. And the very next day, when I went out for a walk in the fragrant morning air—they have a purer, more alive and invigorating air there than anywhere else ("ozone," I said to myself, as I walked along)—it seemed to me that a powerful, gentle hand was lifting me up and carrying me. I was like the sailing boats I saw leaving the harbor, their hulls shining in the first rays of the sun, all their white sails set, stretched and swelling to a favorable wind.

It was in this state of benign ravishment, and without

any ulterior motive, at least, it seemed so to me, that, having wandered for a long time through my favorite streets, those peaceful, intimate, gentle little streets to be found in northern cities, I made slowly for the museum.

I know now that the ambivalence I spoke of was already there, hidden away, without a doubt, in the excitement I felt as I climbed the steps of the museum, an excitement in which a slight apprehension mingled with excessive cheerfulness—a feeling somewhat similar to that of a lover hastening to his first tryst.

The galleries were silent and deserted. A delicate, ashen light flowed from the glass ceilings onto the wide, glossy floors. I walked slowly about, drinking it all in, making long stops before my favorite canvases.

Here, too, one had only to let oneself go and take what was offered. All effort, all doubt, all anxiety, had now been overcome and were things of the past; the goal had been reached. The pictures let me share the fertile, grave serenity of their peaceful smile, the exquisite grace of their detachment. Their lines, each one of which seemed to be unique among all possible lines, miraculously chosen and come upon through some supernatural, unhoped-for stroke of luck, entered into me and set me right. I was tense and vibrant, like the taut string of a bow.

Nevertheless, from time to time, I already felt, coming through the open door of the little passageway in which I knew it was hung, little whiffs that, in the very pure air I was now breathing, were like the puffs of stale, hot air that rise from the ground into the dry, cold air of winter and suddenly envelop us when we walk on the grating above a *metro*. But I felt in no way upset. I was entirely

83

readjusted, scoured clean, afraid of nothing. With the result that when I started towards it, I felt no haste and, it seemed to me, had no motive other than the simple curiosity of the disinterested picture lover who wants to compare his impression with that carried away from earlier visits of some years back. There it was, still in the same place, in the most dimly lighted corner of the passage. I had no need to go up to it in order to decipher on the little gold plate, gleaming in the half-light, the familiar title: *Portrait of a Man Unknown*. I recalled that the picture was not signed: the painter, too, was unknown.

This time it seemed to me, if anything, even more curious than it had before. The lines of the face, the lace jabot and waistcoat, as also the hands, seemed to present the kind of fragmentary, uncertain outlines that the hesitant fingers of a blind man might come upon haltingly, feeling his way. It was as though all effort, all doubt, all anxiety had been overtaken by a sudden catastrophe, and had remained congealed in action, like corpses that have petrified in the position they were in when death overtook them. The eyes alone seemed to have escaped the catastrophe and achieved fulfillment. It was as though they had attracted and concentrated in themselves all the intensity, all the life that was lacking in the still formless, dislocated features. In fact they seemed not quite to belong to this face; they made one think of the eyes of those enchanted beings in fairy tales in whose bodies princes and princesses are held captive by a charm. Their distressing, insistent entreaty made one strangely aware of his silence and the tragedy of it.

As before, but with even greater force, the man's expression gripped me by its determination and authoritativeness. There was no doubt about it, his entreaty was addressed to me, and to me alone; in vain, in order to keep from slipping all the way down the slope I felt I was now on, I told myself that this was a reappearance of introversion, that I had come there like a criminal drawn back by a morbid impulse to the scene of his crime, that I had been led on by an inner need to play a dangerous, unhealthy game with myself; in vain, I tried with all my might, as I always do, to restrain myself, so as to remain on solid ground, on the safe side; out of the blackness of his struggle I felt him making a painful effort to communicate to me his impassioned, stubborn entreaty.

And little by little, I became aware that a timid note, an almost forgotten strain from long ago, had sounded within me, at first, hesitantly. And it seemed to me, as I stood there before him, lost, dissolved in him, that this faltering note, this timid response he had awakened in me, penetrated him and reverberated inside him, that he seized it and gave it back to me increased and magnified as though by an amplifier; it began to rise from him and from me, louder and louder, a song filled with hope that lifted me up and bore me along. . . . As I ran like someone being carried, pushed, even, out of the museum, I saw the attendants lounging on their benches in the corners sit up and look at me sleepily, and outside, on the square, I saw white birds rise on joyous wing at my approach.

Suddenly I felt free. Liberated. The Unknown Man—I said to myself as I dashed up the hotel stairs—"The Man with the Waistcoat," as I called him, had liberated me. Like a blowtorch, the flame that burned inside him had melted the chain by which they had held me in leash. I was free. The cables were cut. I was sailing along, headed for the open sea.

The world stretched out before me like the fields in fairy tales on which, as a result of a few magic words, the traveler sees fine linen covered with delicious viands spread out before him on glistening grass, beside a spring, or along the banks of a stream.

No longer would I have to stretch out a docile hand to be fed by them, to receive from them the little mouthfuls of premasticated foods and ready-to-serve pleasures that they used to give me.

I had retrieved my own foods, my own pleasures, prepared for me alone, and known to me alone. I recognized their former savor. They enveloped me with their mild fragrance, similar to that given forth by wet young leaves in the spring air.

My fetishes. My little gods. The altars on which I had

once laid so many secret offerings, back in the days when I still had all my strength, all my purity.

Scattered about the world, they constituted, for me alone, the means of finding my way. There existed a pact between them and me, a secret alliance. Like the Unknown Man they offered me their support.

They were, above all—these treasures of mine—stones, fragments of walls: gleaming bits of life that I had succeeded in capturing. There were all kinds: certain ones that I knew well, and others that had just greeted me once, that had undulated for me with a soft, warm luster, for one brief moment, as I passed by in a group of people, without being able to stop. But I haven't forgotten them.

As, for instance, in the deserted courtyard of a mosque, the rim of a well, lying warm and golden in the sunlight, downy as a ripe peach, and buzzing with the constant hum of bees on the wing. Its uneven outlines must have been modeled long ago, with delicate, devout tenderness, and then, it has been touched each day by hands accustomed to making quiet gestures and, like people who have had a sheltered childhood, it is as though the stones had been impregnated with all this tenderness and were radiating it even now, as though they gave forth this tenderness like a very gentle glow.

There are also, elsewhere, old stones that are a dark gray, damp and velvety, partly covered by a thin growth of bright green moss. They are sunk deep in the water of the canal, only to reappear here and there, now dull and almost black, now sparkling in the sunlight. The lapping of the water against them is gentle and caressing like the name Tiepolo, when spoken very softly: *Tie-po-lo,* which calls up patches of deep-blue sky and winged colors.

I recall, too, along tortuous, roughly paved little streets, certain bits of wall that are bathed in light. Occasionally the deep shade of a palm branch serves to heighten their brilliance.

And in the north there are wharves that are a silvery white in the morning light, and corners of wharves along canals where silver-winged birds fly, and whitewashed walls, snow-bordered, which, at dusk, take on the shade of blue-rinsed linen, the way snow does.

They sprang up around me from every side, my gems and delights of old, more vivid, more radiant than they had ever been.

It seemed to me that during our long separation all their sap which was intended for me had collected in them. They were heavier and riper than before, all swollen with their unused sap. I felt their firm, warm nearness, I leaned on them and they gave me protection; in their proximity I felt like a fruit ripening in the sun, I, too, became heavy and swollen with sap, buzzing with promises and impulses and entreaties.

As it had done before, long ago, the future stretched ahead of me, deliciously indistinct and blurred, hazy as a mist-covered horizon on the morning of a fine day.

Like water that divides under the prow of a ship, time began gently to open up, in a moment of endless expansion, under the pressure of my hopes and my desires.

The water opened with a sound of crumpled silk under the bow of the boat. Fine crests of white foam raced by, trembling with delight. . . .

89

"That will do! Be quiet! That will do!" A gray-suited form rose, and a rounded back leaned over the table. A fist could be heard coming down with such force that the tea cups quivered: "That will do! Be quiet! I know it!" As he shouted this he struck a heavy blow on the table.

It was funny how little impression that had made on me, how I had not reacted at the time. A mutual friend of long standing, a woman I had met quite by chance, had just happened to tell me about it. "That will do! Be quiet!" People had started and begun to stare at them—he had shouted so loudly—and everybody was terribly embarrassed, as always when he indulged in one of his unaccountable vagaries, in public.

She had laughed indulgently in telling me about it, because he was charming, wasn't he, when he wanted to be; when you knew him well, there was nobody who could be more delightful or more attractive than he, when he was at his best, and I, too, had laughed indulgently, I hadn't reacted at all, as often happens, when certain words seem to glance off us like that, without leaving a trace: we pass them over with a smile, as I had done, quite obliviously. But words enter into us without our knowledge, they take deep root in us, and then, it may be long afterwards, they suddenly rise up in us and force us to stop all at once, in the middle of the street, or else they wake us at night, with a start that leaves us sitting straight up in bed, filled with apprehension.

At present, these words had risen up in me; as unconsciously as the bee carries pollen from one plant to another, our old friend had implanted them in me and they had gradually begun to grow there, they had slowly ripened in

90

the gentle warmth in which I myself had recently been blossoming forth, they had grown in me like a fruit stone, and already I was beginning to feel their cutting edges inside me: "That will do! Be quiet! That will do!" He had shouted that at me, I knew it perfectly well. It was in opposition to me, in order to challenge me that he had shouted—in a fit of helpless rage and defiance. He must have sensed vaguely that these words were going to reach me, that it was towards me and, above all, at me that these words had been let fly like an entreaty or like a challenge. I am sure he must have sensed it. I know him. Underneath his every action, even the apparently trivial and innocuous ones, there is a sort of wrong side, another facet, a hidden one, known only to us, and which is turned in my direction. It is through this, no doubt, that he attracts me and continues to have such a strong hold over me.

For some time already, he has certainly been trying to get my dander up, taunting me gently, in that insidious way of his, or teasing me, while he sits there taking life easy: "Still traveling, eh? Works of art? Museums? The Uffizi? Rembrandt, eh? Or Tiepolo? And what about canals? And pigeons? As for me, I go to Evian. Ever hear of it? Hotel Royal. Not at all bad. And a magnificent view. . . ."

Seated on the hotel terrace, in a comfortable, cushion-filled wicker chair, while the orchestra plays his favorite tunes, he gives me a sly wink: "What are people after anyway? What more do they want, when they can be so comfortable. . . ?" Spread out before him, "the view" offers its rounded croup in an agreeable display. Haystacks dotting the fields in regular rows gleam in the sunlight as though they had been polished. The kind of music that is intended for dance halls, for Sunday afternoon concerts in winter, or for evenings at the opera, a heavy, luxurious, upholstered kind of music, fills the air about him, then rolls away over fields and haystacks and pine trees, keeping the view in its place, at a respectful distance.

The music wraps him about, it protects him, as does also the double row of geraniums planted around the edge of the terrace. Here is the rampart behind which he takes cover, the vantage point from which he can watch me with a taunting eye, running after new "sensations" or "aesthetic visions," eh? The Uffizi? as he says. For his part, however, he doesn't need all that. He's easily satisfied. He is able to fashion according to his will, and to dominate, the things about him, he is able to keep them at a distance, instead of clinging to them and living off them in the position of a trembling, flabby larva, or a parasite.

This, I am sure, is what he is trying to make me understand and feel, as he sits there comfortably reading his newspaper, chatting with friends, listening to the music, taking it easy in the sunshine on the terrace of the Hotel Royal. Each gesture he makes, his very presence there, constitutes a sly provocation, a challenge.

It must have boiled up little by little and then suddenly spurted out to the great astonishment of everybody. They had gone out for a walk after the afternoon nap, as they did every day. This time they had even had an objective; they were going for a drink of the famous hot chocolate made with cream, to be had at the fashionable dairy farm.

It was to be a real expedition and they were quite excited. They had even been obliged to take walking sticks, the road was so poor in places. But it was fun, the women laughed as they teetered along on their narrow white-kid heels, while the gentlemen held them gallantly by the elbow to guide them over the rough spots. Everybody was in fine feather when they arrived, a bit tired, of course, but it was the kind of tiredness that would be good for them. He would sleep all the better, his friends told him, he ought to bestir himself a bit, he was growing too indolent. They were happy, just a wee bit hungry, but a cup of delicious chocolate with crisp rolls was waiting for them. . . .

And it was here, under these orange parasols planted in the thick, gleaming grass like the flame-colored mushrooms that dot the fields in children's picture books; it was here, while they were all seated at their little table, surrounded by waitresses dressed up like Trianon dairymaids, in the midst of all these smart turkeys and roosters, that it had happened.

Was it the kind of depression that occasionally follows excitement, was it the heat? Was it a sort of vague disquiet, a vague feeling of resentment at being there, a sense of waste and emptiness? Or was it some distant effluvia, a sort of remote challenge emanating, perhaps, from me? Was it the kind of oppressive uneasiness he pretends to ignore, but which he always feels in luxurious, flashy or stilted surroundings? Or was it the kindly humoring of his friends, which always reacts on him the way a too weak show of gentleness on the part of the person who looks after it reacts on a nervous child? I really don't know; but he suddenly felt impelled to make a scene, to break all that up and rip it apart; perhaps, too—this is not impossible, he's such a bundle of contradictions; despite his attitude of defiance and hatred, it's not improbable—he may have felt impelled to leap beyond the polished fields, to tear himself away from that benumbing music, and join me. He, too, suddenly felt himself in the clutches, in the grip of some-one who was taunting him from a distance; something inside him, like a kernel, had suddenly become hard and heavy. It was something in him, perhaps, in these artificial surroundings, in the emptiness of the afternoon, during this long period of deadening leisure—at times, one had the sensation of swallowing against one's will, or inhaling with all one's might, a sort of thick, sweetish substance that produced a feeling of stuffiness and buzzing, rather like being under an anaesthetic—it was perhaps a sudden throbbing inside him that indicated a return to life, his own life, a feeling that brought him somehow closer to me, without his knowing why, and which impelled him to get up and brandish it—his life—before his astonished, fright-ened friends, who tried to quiet him.

It must have started in a rather insidious way, by easy stages: the sort of commonplace conversation that takes place over a tea table.

They must have asked him (they know how pleased he always is when people take an interest in him) how his children were passing their holidays, particularly his daughter, and he had sensed right away, like an irritating itch, the exasperating contrast between this contrived set-ting, as shiny as a pretty toy, and what had begun to unfold within him—his grievances, his daughter, his life. With only a faint show of annoyance, he had replied at first, the way one lightly scratches a mosquito bite, that she was away, traveling; that she was traveling in Corsica . . . and then just the word Corsica had started it boiling inside him, his voice had grown deeper and somewhat harsh; his head lowered and his slightly red dewlaps drooped. He began to drum on the table, his eye fixed malevolently on the waitresses rigged out like comic opera peasant girls, who danced smiling attendance, as they simperingly poured the chocolate.

Despite the fact that these old friends of his had known him for so long, they had never learned to foresee his reactions, which remained unpredictable and unaccountable for them. They continued to question him gently, in the belief that it pleased him, accustomed as they were to going ahead with words, in set phrases, like horses with blinkers on, who follow the beaten track, without ever seeing anything of what surrounds them other than what is accepted, obvious. They questioned him the way one always does when one wants to be polite and give people pleasure, about his children . . . his daughter. . . . She liked to travel. . . . And how long would she remain away? And then, mysteriously attracted (the way one slides down a slope, or falls into space) by his sullen, slightly threatening silence, they had probably said: "These days children are certainly spoiled; if we had asked our parents to travel about like that. . . ." And something had begun to throb hard inside him, it had given a bound and spurted out (reminding them of the princess from whose mouth toads fell when she spoke), it had spurted out and was rolling along before their eyes, a toad sprawling there on the tablecloth

among the cups of chocolate, or rolling along the ground, in
the field: "But that doesn't satisfy them. . . . She wanted to
go to Spain, in spite of the present exchange. The present
exchange. As if I could afford that. But one of her friends
was going there. . . . I said to her: 'Why not China?' " He
was laughing: Ho-ho! a pointed sort of laughter in which
there was a last remaining trace of good nature; that hateful, uneasy, false laughter of his. "Ho-ho! Why not China?
Her outfit alone would have cost about seven or eight
thousand francs." They looked surprised—he could have
bitten them he was so raving mad, he would have liked to
seize all of them together and snatch them away from
this loud luxury which he hated, and these surroundings
which exasperated him, into which he had stupidly allowed
himself to be dragged by them, to punish them. "Absolutely; the outfit alone. . . ." He stared before him, stubborn and filled with resentment. . . . "Absolutely, that's
how it is. . . . Absolutely. . . ." They tried clumsily to
calm him by assuming a tone of incredulity. "Oh! your
figure must be a bit high. . . ." It was then that he had
stood up, filled with rage, lifted his fist and, shouting,
banged it down on the table—he let himself go with them,
they were the kind, like myself, with whom people like him
fly into a rage, they didn't know how to hold him back—he
had shouted: "That will do! I know it! That's how it is."
And they had started up, they had turned to see if people
at the other tables had heard him, which was a sign of
weakness on their part that brought him to the point of
white heat: "That will do! Be quiet! I know them. They're
like that. That's how it is. There's never enough to please
them. They're never satisfied. All alike. I know them.

There's never enough. The moon . . . China. . . ." He threw everything into one, the too dainty waitresses, the people around him sitting like motionless dolls at their little tables in their too new, too stiff clothes, the friends who had dragged him there and were forcing him to stay there when what he felt like doing, he too, perhaps, was to be somewhere else, all alone, surrounded by the things he loved, to go away . . . and lastly his daughter and myself who were defying him now from afar, strutting about somewhere at his expense, parasitically, going into ecstasies before "masterpieces," somewhere gaping at church portals or at fragments of famous columns, flouting him and running him down.

*I*t's a good sign, apparently, a sign of recovery, when a patient breaks away from his doctor and feels no further need to lean on him. In this respect, I seemed indeed to have recovered. I could no longer think of my specialist without a feeling of aversion mingled with revulsion. It was hard for me to understand how I could have been so weak as to turn to him for help. This was not, however—and I did not mistake it as such—a sign of independence or strength. All I had done was to change masters. Now it was the Unknown Man, the "Man with Doublet," who held the leash at the other end of which I was walking. Oh, it was a very gentle tie, but perhaps all the more dangerous for my independence in that I felt not the slightest desire to be free from it.

The Unknown Man served as a sort of screen; he protected me. With the result that the treacherous blow the old man had just aimed at me so tellingly from his distant dairy farm was deadened before it reached me. It seemed to me that it had struck me only on the rebound, after having first hit the "Man with Doublet." Something that came from him, a slight something torn from him in passing, his vague cool fragrance, reached me at the same time as the usual anguish, the old hatred. The Unknown Man shared my torment. I was no longer alone. A comforting feeling of confidence and dignity, even of pride, sustained me as I started on my return journey.

The old man's outcry, the challenge he had hurled at me, made my departure seem urgent; I was impatient, too, to confront him, to match my strength with his, now that I felt I was being upheld. Of course I told myself that this was probably nothing but cunning on my part, an excuse of my own invention in order to justify my old morbid leanings, to give in to my former aberrations and slip remorselessly into the gaping abyss which they always open up before me, and into which I fall in their pursuit. I was nevertheless obliged to recognize, in all impartiality, that something had changed.

A new delight, that still smacked strongly of forbidden pleasures, but akin to the joy I felt when I went back again to my fetishes, to the objects of my cult, a delight that recalled that other, very soft delight that I felt in the presence of velvety stones caressed by gently lapping water, or at the sight of sun-bathed walls at the end of little mauve-shadowed streets, a hitherto unknown joy prevailed over my usual anguish, as I left to join them. I would see their setting again: the wan grass plots bordered with box hedge, the little petrified city squares, and the lifeless façades of the houses with their impersonal, absent appearance, the look they have of not wanting to attract attention, or enter into contact, or offer any sort of hold, as though they feared lest a too insistent gaze bring forth into the open something crouching behind their walls, something which, in spite of themselves, they secrete and contain. There was also in my delight something of the comfortable egotism, the secret pride of the rich man who takes pleasure in walking through squalid neighborhoods, or visiting the Flea Market, while relishing the sharp contrast they present with the luxurious background he has just come from and to which he will soon return. As I saw it all again, I experienced this same sort of delectable contrast with the treasures I had just left behind, and which were still present in me, the same agreeable impression of blissful security and airy unconcern.

And it was doubtless in order to increase my joy a bit, to lend spice to my pleasure that, the very next day after my arrival, I went prowling about, somewhat at random, in the suburbs. I found myself in a place that reminded me of certain settings of my childhood, narrow, gritty looking houses, vague in color, fronted by dusty little gardens planted with shrubs trimmed in the shape of pagodas or birds, and all of them surrounded by the same black fencing bordered with box hedge.

I wandered about for a long while, lingering in certain particularly dull, benumbed little streets, with a funny

101

feeling of satisfaction that smacked of the slightly dubious: a very intimate, soft feeling of withdrawal into oneself, accompanied, or rather heightened, by the vague impression of doing something people disapproved of . . . and also a sort of confused excitement.

My excitement changed into anxious waiting—still this mixture of apprehension and hope—as I climbed the steps of the station on my way back. I stood for a while on the footbridge above the tracks, leaning on the railing and looking with close attention at the drab gray platform over which floated acrid, sulphur-reeking smoke and, behind it, the avenue leading down to the station, a gloomy avenue bordered on each side with pebbly houses and little gardens with mutilated trees. I was all agog. It seemed to me that I was bearing down on it all, that I was pressing it, the way we press a fruit to extract the juice, with all my might.

As usual, before I even noticed them I sensed their presence. For it made the atmosphere grow vibrant and dense, as though held firm and taut in a violent effort to eject them from it.

And again this time, I had an impression of something faked or miraculous, such as people must have when they watch the performance of certain fakirs, in India, who throw that rope of theirs into the air, while an entire bemused crowd watches as the rope stands upright, straight and stiff as the trunk of a palm tree.

They were walking slowly along the platform and, like Moses in his cloudy pillar, they appeared to me to be entirely wrapped in the sulphurous smoke from the train that had just passed. Extremely stagy as always. So stagy, so made up, in fact, that they themselves seemed unreal, impossible. Characters making their entrance on stage. I remained leaning on the footbridge railing, my heart thumping. It was the same emotion as before, whenever I saw them, but mingled, this time, with a feeling of satisfaction, of pride; that of the fakir who has successfully performed his act.

They were walking along the platform: he with his hunched-up back under his worn overcoat, looking a bit shrunken (he did it on purpose, I know: getting old, eh? That's how life is . . . youth, eh? middle age . . .), he was also wearing his old worn hat, the one he usually wears on outings of this kind, when he goes to see his very old friends, those for whom he doesn't "make any fuss," with whom "he feels perfectly at home, . . ." he had known them for such a long time. The old woman walking beside him, to whom he had offered his arm, was his friend's wife. . . . I recognized her, it was she all right; she had aged, she too had shrunk; she was wearing a black plush coat that was so worn it had reddish tints as if it were rusty; she was carrying a bundle, a sort of shopping bag, it must have been a plain black oilcloth bag, I couldn't see very well—the footbridge rises high above the platform and I couldn't see well on account of the smoke and the people walking on the platform, who kept getting in my way—I guessed it rather, if only because of the warm-heartedness, the air of solicitous comprehension with which he took the bundle from her hands and set it down on the ground between them in front of the bench when they sat down side by side, waiting for their train.

He loved that, I know, the homely black oilcloth bundle and the worn old coat, and the dirty platform filled with sulphur fumes, the houses, the little gardens: it was in order to get a whiff of that, to inhale it all with that dubious, sweetish sensuality that we feel when we sniff our own odors, that he had come here. Somewhat as I myself had done.

He had felt all exhilarated before taking the train, at the moment when his ticket was handed to him and he read the name of the station on the little third-class gray card. In the compartment, he had remained huddled up to himself, relishing it all in advance, filled with a funny sort of satisfaction that he would not have been able to analyze, and he had felt quite cheerful when, on the way out, as he gave up his ticket, he saw, in front of the station, the dusty avenue bordered with little gray gardens and, on the gate of one of them, just opposite the station, the cracked name plate he knew so well (for thirty years it had showed the same crack), bearing the following inscription in gold letters: *Doctor of Medicine. Tuesday. Thursday. Saturday.* He too, probably, had had the same feeling of mild excitement, of expectancy, of delightful withdrawal from everything as he pushed open the gate, crossed the garden and pressed his finger to the doorbell.

From time to time he needs to come and rub up against all that, he needs to come and sniff it, there's certainly something about it that excites him and gives him a sensation similar to that of the wealthy bourgeois walking through the Flea Market, or perhaps an impression of timorous evasion, a somewhat embarrassed, furtive gesture of self-assurance the sort of contentment experienced by those who give in to a secret vice.

Certainly, in the same way that I had come bearing my

treasures with me, he had come with, in the back of his mind, the gleaming well-polished lawn of the dairy farm, the pier beside the lake where he took his morning strolls, all clean and sweet smelling in his well-pressed suit, reading his newspaper in the sunlight, treating the girls, daughters of his friends, without regard to cost—he'll always buy anything under those circumstances: a pretty salesgirl smiling at him delightedly—flowers, bunches of cyclamen or violets.

When he's with other people, he likes to remain a bit aloof like that, without their noticing it, to assume secretly a dual personality and get a taste, without, above all, ever revealing anything, of that marvelous freedom that will permit him, whenever he wants, to change both role and setting, whereas they will remain there indefinitely, faced with the dreary little gardens on the drowsy little square.

They were making the trip together, doubtless she had some errand to do in Paris, and so took advantage of the occasion to travel with him.

How thoughtful he was of her. . . . There he was moving the bundle—he must have relished all these precautions, all that respectfulness—so that no one should trample on it. . . . His gestures showed such satisfaction, were so full of affectionate solicitude. . . . Now he moved over towards her a bit, in order to make room for a little old man who had just sat down beside him.

They sat there motionless, all dark and opaque in the smoke. They didn't move, sitting there side by side, he bent somewhat forward, both hands resting on the head of his cane, and she, leaning back against the seat, her hands folded in her lap, a vague look in her eyes. I leaned over, waiting, filled with impatience and revulsion. It seemed to me that I was gently poking a stick at inert animals to see if they would move.

He sat huddled up against her, he felt good and warm up against her; in that drabness he loved, he was inhaling with delight the sulphurous smell.

I leaned straining over the parapet, my entire energy straining so tensely in their direction that I felt I should break in two.

There was something that excited and exasperated me as though someone was taking pleasure in teasing me, the way you tease a dog by fondling its nose with a bone or a lump of sugar. It was an idea—still very vague—that tickled me like that. At times I seemed to have got it and was holding on to it, and then it would elude me again. What had first set me on its track was the black oilcloth bundle: already an intuition, a presentiment, had attracted my attention to that bundle, and above all, to the solicitous way he had taken the bundle from her hands. But here there was something else besides solicitude—there was profound respect, veneration: in the presence of this bundle he was capable of taking off his hat and kneeling. The cracked plate, the scraggy shrubs, the whole shabby, pinched setting, these are his fetishes, the objects of his cult: "hard necessity," probably . . . "sad reality" . . . concerning which they never jest. . . . But it seemed to me that he was play-acting (a train hid them from me, not their train, fortunately, and it didn't stop: I was so afraid they were going to elude me just at the moment when I was there trying my best to see them, to bring them into the very center of my focus)—he was playing, that was certain: a funny, morbid game . . . it amused him to fondle this Reality, to touch it lightly. . . . That was what gave him pleasure, to disport himself a bit like this on its surface. The same pleasure, doubtless, the same hidden satisfaction that he experiences sometimes at funerals as he watches the coffin sink to the bottom of the hole and listens to the sound of the little handfuls of earth falling on the wooden top.

He loves that, he loves to come like that from time to time and kiss the hem of their goddess's garment (his and his daughter's goddess): they resemble each other.

Only he was playing a dangerous game. She was all-powerful, the old woman who was with him—a vestal of the cult. She was wearing all the sacred emblems: the old toque and the rusty plush coat, the oilcloth bundle, and the general attitude: hands folded in her lap, a humble, resigned look, and the face: the placid expression of docile approval, as she nodded away. Her word was all-powerful. And yet she seemed to be, like those chosen by the Divinity to carry out sacred missions, purity, innocence itself.

I saw her turn towards him: it was evident that she was aware of nothing, in her eyes he was nothing but an old friend who was a good, decent sort underneath his churlish ways, "a rough diamond:" she was so innocent, so credulous, that she had always accepted him in this role which was the one he had chosen to play with her and her husband; she was undoubtedly asking him news of himself—"he has a hard time, poor fellow, he's so alone, really"—she was asking him questions . . . how was his heating, perhaps, or how was he making out? The last time he had said that his furnace wasn't working, or about his maid . . . whether she got well again, or about his daughter . . . she seemed to have heard somebody say that he was worried about money, investments that had turned out badly . . . I couldn't tell, but it seemed to me that I saw her—like the game in which, blindfolded, we look for a hidden object—pat him a bit here and there as though trying to find something, a sensitive spot . . . as I leaned over them, I felt like shouting: "You're warm, no, no, you're cold, now you're hot, burning hot!" He fidgeted, slightly out of patience, reared back, shook his head like a bull when the banderillas are stuck behind its ears, this time she was "burning" . . . his daughter, he was answering her (his voice must have been very low, almost stifled): "Still the same, she'll never change, you know that, there's no changing her . . ." now the old woman was right up against him, but she didn't see anything, she was innocence itself: "What? At her age, she still makes demands on you . . . ? Why, she's getting on . . . at her age, people have more pride than that . . . she's old enough to be a grandmother . . . it's high time she understood something about life, she should learn that we weren't put here to amuse ourselves. . . ." He hung his head, he was suffocating, he murmured an assent that expressed his helplessness: "Of course, but that's how it is. . . ." His voice had grown hoarse. . . . It seemed to him as if the old woman were passing her hands over his wounds, he felt like shouting, but she didn't notice anything. . . . Innocently she pronounced the sacred words: "They're not kind to you. . . ."

I didn't see his reaction, the train was coming, they rose, I saw him pick up the bundle and push her towards the third-class carriages. They got on. She must have sat down, and he, obliged to stand up in the very crowded suburban train, had the impression that his game had turned out

badly, he had been too close to the abyss . . . he had slipped
. . . the old woman had pushed him into it . . . he hated
her now—what business was it of hers? The smelly train
upset him; it seemed to him that the grubby houses, the
dusty box plants, the entire shabby suburb, had left a sedi-
ment on him that irritated him the way stickiness on the
hands and face does. He was in a hurry to get away from
it all, to get back home.

Once they've reached the Denfert Station, he will have
pulled himself together a bit, he'll shake her hand in his
rough-diamond manner: "Well, I'll see you soon, eh? See
you soon. Thanks. Thanks." in a voice that has recovered its
tone. And she will say shyly, to console him (it's so sad, that
lonely life of his): "And don't you worry, you hear me." He
will shrug his shoulders with that occasional smile of his,
that slightly childish smile, uncomfortable and abashed,
which his friends like about him, which sometimes makes
him irresistible, and which she will be touched by. I myself am touched by it.

This will be the picture she will retain of him: this face
seen in half profile—a vague sketch with barely indicated
lines, from which stand out more clearly the contours of
the cheek that, seen from this angle, has something naïve
about it, something that has remained intact as in the case
of a very young man—and the abashed, touching smile,
like a child's.

And he, while he shakes her hand, will feel that, in spite
of himself, he is getting like this picture, that he is a faithful reflection of it: it is this extreme awareness of the impression others have of him, this capacity to reproduce like
a mirror the picture of himself that people give back to

109

him, that always gives him the painful, slightly disturbing sensation of play-acting with everybody, of never being "himself:" "a frequent trait," my specialist would say, "of nervous persons."

The picture that he was reproducing just now, that of the "childlike, naïve philosopher who is defenseless before life," restored his self-assurance. He felt all right again. Indeed he had the faculty of straightening up like that quickly. But if I were to stand directly in front of him, right in the middle of the street, and shout in his face: "So it turned out badly, did it, that expedition of yours . . . to go and get a whiff of sordidness . . . ? The old woman spoiled everything . . . you remember . . . there on the bench . . . when you were waiting for the train?" I believe that he would be sincere if he replied that he understood nothing, absolutely nothing of such mad talk: they never do understand when you bowl them over with truths of this sort, he no more than the rest of them, as for that, he's like them, or else he forces himself to be like them, I don't know, one never knows with him he's so sly, always double-faced, always play-acting, with himself as well. But I do know, in any case, that I'd come back empty-handed if I ever dared to try anything like that with him.

It's their way of defending themselves, with all of them, as I said before, this sort of unawareness, whether sincere or pretended. They curl up like hedgehogs when danger becomes too great, close all exits and allow these "truths" of mine, which I hatch so lovingly, to bounce against them without penetrating the surface.

Standing before his door, on the landing, he would shake his head with the indulgent, amused air that an adult might assume as he recalls the disconnected prattle of a child: "What's that story? What's all that wild talk? All those silly stories?" He would shake his head, while calmly choosing his latchkey from the bunch spread out on his hand, he would shrug his shoulders; already, in his memory, the adventure corresponded to the label it had worn to start with: a visit that he had already put off too long . . . but he had to make up his mind one day, you can't neglect old friends like that, friends with whom you have so many memories in common, ah! it doesn't make us feel any younger, thirty-five years already since he had first met her, what am I saying, thirty-five years, in another year it will be exactly forty years since he saw her for the first time, she was still quite young then: "I got myself some black glasses, would you like to see them? I don't want to miss the eclipse of the sun," he remembered as if it were yesterday the way, when she said that, she had screwed up her nose, which she still does at times, he had been struck by the way she had said that the first time he saw her. . . . Well, well, all that's a long time ago, we've all changed considerably since, but just the same, it's nice to see old friends, you feel at ease with them, perfectly at home, it's like wearing old clothes; but it was awfully hot in the train, it's a tiring trip in those crowded suburban trains, another time he would do better to leave earlier, or else later, and accept their invitation to stay for dinner, otherwise the return trip was really exhausting. . . . That's what he would tell himself, this is always the way they retire within themselves, like snails that retract right away as soon as you lift a finger to touch them, draw in their horns and sink deep into their shells. That's what he said, surely, as soon as he

111

had reached home, shut his door, laid his hat on the hall table, and thrown his overcoat on the bench.

He sank into his armchair, the one he usually sits in, behind his desk, and grew motionless, staring before him, his paunch thrust forward. A great flabby heavy mass. Suddenly I felt very small, even tiny, beside him; his great bloated mass took up all the room, flattened me out against the wall. And it seemed to me now, as he sat there without moving, that I was like Tom Thumb beside him, spying, terrified, on the sleeping Giant.

Stockily ensconced in his armchair, he was reading a little bound book picked up off his desk; he read with effort, fidgeting impatiently in his chair. . . . I know, I saw him, I remember having met him one time starting on his morning walk with one of these little books in his hand, he showed it to me with a rather mocking, satisfied smile: "Oh, just something extremely simple, childish even, a plain textbook, a primer-school book on arithmetic. . . ." I saw how amused he was by my astonishment. . . . "Yes, indeed, it's one of my favorite pastimes, reading school books. You know they're very well written. Excellent. It's extremely interesting to see the way children are taught these things nowadays. Not so simple as people think, either"—he stared before him with that faraway look of his —"not simple at all if you really think about it, if you take the trouble to go into it a bit. . . ."

He resumed his reading at the page he had been studying in the morning before he went to take the train: the chapter on division. . . . As comforting to the eye of the besieger as a citadel that hoists the white flag, the rule of three had surrendered to him completely, had revealed to him, after gasps of vain resistance, its ultimate secrets. He felt his mind tauten and crack with the effort required to triturate the hard, impenetrable subject matter constituted by the rule of three . . . the four operations, fractions. . . .

This is what he practices on, it's on this that he sharpens his pincers and mandibles. As for him, he needs so little, a simple class book meant for a child of twelve suffices for him—it's only a poor workman, he loves to repeat, who complains of poor tools—as far as he is concerned, he needs so little, a few exercises every day, a few good gymnastic exercises to maintain in form and keep lithe and in perfect condition, always ready for use, this highly perfected instrument, this powerful apparatus that nature has given him, thanks to which he has been able to attain after so many years, to the desirable, privileged position that is his. . . . Now I know what always made me think, when I saw him seated at his table without moving, that he was like a big motionless spider in its web. It was not only because of the look he has of waiting for his prey when he sits there withdrawn into himself, but also because of his position: in the center—he is in the center, he sits there in state, dominating everything—and the entire universe is like a web of his own weaving, which he drapes at will about himself.

As he sits there, motionless, he has more and more, with the passing years, an impression of freedom and power.

He doesn't need to move a finger. He has only to want it, and anything, any one of the objects that so long as he has not subjected them to his scrutiny, remain quaking and hesitant on the outer edge of existence, let him take hold of it, any one of them, the inkwell, the paperweight, let him examine it closely—and immediately, what a transformation. . . . Does there exist a work of art—let no one come and talk to me about Poussin or Chardin—why get excited, why chase through museums? . . . as for him, he never goes near them, he doesn't have to, when all we need to do is to look closely at that bit of worn carpet, there under the window, in the sunlight, or at that lamp, or that inkstand, that sheet of white paper on the table. . . . What painter could ever depict this mystery, this wonder, this miracle. . . .

Occasionally, when he's seated there at his table, he likes to amuse himself by picking up at random just anything, the most unobtrusive, most insignificant of objects which he hoists up from out of its nothingness, holds a few seconds, trembling with life, under his all-powerful gaze, then lets drop. And as I lie in wait there in my corner, flattened out, he has only to look in my direction for me to become— like that time on the stairway—a moth struggling madly in the blinding glare of headlights, or rather for me to become, under his gaze, like an ant that he would be amused to watch for a few moments, as it scurries busily about, comically bending its every effort to lift something that is quite evidently too heavy. He would let me go soon, I should not hold his attention for long. I interest him too little. He has other, more interesting pastimes, that are infinitely more profitable, other more absorbing games.

He has only to stretch out his hand and there within reach, agreeably presented, stripped of vain ornament, reduced to essentials—he doesn't need to bother with details, essentials suffice for him, he has no time to lose, the entire world is his—there, neatly arranged so as to entice and hold him, contained in those little books scattered about on his desk, those little salmon-colored books that are so convenient, just look, you can put them in your pocket if you want to take them with you when you go for a walk; there they are, within reach—he has only to stretch out his hand—the most recent researches and discoveries, the most scholarly, the most daring theories and systems: great fellows they are, he takes pleasure in recognizing this fact, very brilliant fellows too, he likes to repeat it, as he purses his lips and nods with the air of one who is able to judge. It's often amusing to observe their zealotry, their foregone conclusions, their blind tenaciousness, the blinkers they wear, even the best of them. But he doesn't blame them. He understands. He knows that these limitations and foregone conclusions, this blindness, are all necessary in order for them to create for his use products of the best quality. For him, as he sits there, these little books scattered about on his desk are nothing more than selected instruments with which he works, lenses, or different colored spectacles, through which he obtains each time a different view.

According to his whim, or his humor, according to whether his preference of the moment leans towards one or the other of them, the picture varies. Everything changes. According to his whim. The world, always amenable, grows infinitely vast or, on the contrary, shrinks to nothing: becomes narrow and dark, or immense and transparent. According to his whim, colors change. Nothing is set. Nothing impresses him. Under his impetus, like the frail web in which the spider swings, the world sways and trembles.

115

And little by little, with the passing of the years, as he sits there all alone, he experiences a constantly increasing delightful feeling of security and quietude. A feeling that may be compared to that of the small investor comfortably settled in his neat little bungalow, fixed up to suit his taste, which he has built for his declining years; a satisfaction, as he opens one after the other of the little salmon-colored books, comparable to that of the retired bureaucrat as, when night comes, before going to bed, he makes a tour of inspection, gently presses the pears in the garden, in their paper bags, opens the canisters aligned on the kitchen shelf and peers into them: in this one cinnamon, in that one sugar or coffee. All of it belongs to him. He is in his own home. Secure.

But watch out, I feel that I might be rather tempted to tarry dangerously over this analogy, this aspect of him which he now spreads out before me so accommodatingly: the small investor safe in his neat bungalow, his quietude . . . his feeling of security that increases curiously with age . . . I all but let myself be touched by his detachment, or by his serenity, which is so becoming to old age. A step further and I would be seeing him the way he likes to show himself, bold—he feels so very strong—to the point of daring to face his former anguish, the fear that suddenly used to lacerate him (he often speaks of it) a long time ago, when he was young: taking pleasure in the sensation of a slight pecking, a slight tickle that its blunted point now gives him; roaming about cemeteries as I have sometimes seen him do (he loves this "dreams of a solitary stroller" kind of thing), one of his little books in his hand; relishing the contrasts; listening with pleasure, on a radiant spring morning, to the twitter of birds, somewhat strident in the too great silence; leaning over the tombstones with moved satisfaction in order to read the inscriptions; musing about the possible lives of all these people, this link in the infinite chain, this flash. . . .

If I hadn't restrained myself in time, I was about to glide weakly down this slippery incline, I was about to let myself be caught gently in his toils. With him one must always be on the alert, advance with only the most extreme prudence, and look backwards before taking a step forward. Above all, one must beware of an impression of easy victory which he can give at times, when he accepts a little too willingly, for instance, a frontal attack, with a sort of motionlessness that is so different from the furtive leaps with which he usually escapes, as soon as anybody comes too near him. But I believe that, this time, I succeeded in pulling myself together in time. As in an adventure story, there is always something that comes to my rescue at the last moment.

This time it was a memory from the past that came to extricate me from the state of contented relaxation to which I was lazily about to give in. The recollection of one of those little shows such as he occasionally puts on which, already at the time, had caused me to have serious misgivings.

It was one evening—a beautiful spring evening—I remember. I met him with a friend of his, airing themselves on the boulevard.

They were walking side by side on the middle sidewalk where, between the two rows of sycamores, the air was purer. They were walking slowly, leaning against each other, as though borne along by the sweetish, soft evening air. Almost as though they were holding him on leash, dragging languidly along behind them, a surly expression on his face, was a young man, an adolescent, the friend's son, I believe.

I started to follow them too, walking in silence beside the young man.

They were engaged in discussing their favorite topics of conversation, death, life. . . . They didn't seem to notice us, but I knew—and the surly adolescent certainly knew too —that it was a parade taking place in our honor: "Death," he said to his friend, "life"—and I could feel how he was hugging himself delightedly at the same time that he gave a glance sidewise at the adolescent and myself, to see what effect he was producing—how we magnify these questions when we are young!—". . . the excessive importance"—he waved his arms in the air in a gesture of emphasis—"that is attached to all that, to one's death and to one's life. Now that the end of the entire farce is near, we see that it was nothing really, hardly a moment of consciousness . . . a flash . . . and when you think how few people realize that. They never give it a thought. Out of fear? Or out of inability to take it in? In any case, as for me, who have always regarded it as the unalterable background against which the play is played, I understand better each day how little it all matters, how quickly they're all over, all those dreams of fame and love and happiness that amuse us when we're young. The fact is that for us, eh"—he was smiling with that subtle, disillusioned air of his—"for us, it'll soon be over, the trick will be turned. . . ." The surly adolescent continued to follow them obediently, in silence. Doubtless the halo they had donned fascinated him, or perhaps he hadn't the strength to fight, he was so weak, so frail and defenseless, as a result of the too mild tepid air, the deliquescent softness of that spring evening.

From time to time they would be seen to separate and give each other smacking slaps on the shoulder, with an air of satisfaction, their long black overcoats flapped together, overlapping for a moment, then parted and floated behind them like banners, or flags: "Yes," he was saying, "I used to have a friend who trained his parrot to say about anything whatsoever: 'All of that has really no importance.' Believe me, each one of us, at our age especially, should have a parrot like the one my old friend had." Thus it was that, one evening, I watched him play his apparently harmless, clandestine games, and confident that he would go unpunished, give his furtive slaps, like a cat playing with a mouse.

I remember how the vague sensation of uneasiness that this little scene had caused me, similar to that of painful indigestion, or the coated tongue that results from food of doubtful freshness, suddenly disappeared, and my feeling of relief and joy was so great that I stopped all at once on the edge of the pavement and began to laugh out loud. It hadn't taken with me. In me he had found a too powerful opponent. I laughed out loud, standing there on the pavement's edge. His shot had misfired. And now it was I who was on top, I who was holding the right end of the stick. I had succeeded in piercing the heavy armor with

119

which he had protected himself and behind which he felt safe, and I had caught hold of something alive—his hand, which he held out to me furtively. I had seized his hand on the wing. I held him tight.

In the same way that the blood distends the arteries, throbs in the temples and beats against the eardrums when air pressure is lowered, so, at night, in the rarefied atmosphere engendered by solitude and silence anguish that has been contained during the day swells and weighs upon us; an oppressive mass fills the head and chest, inflates the lungs, presses like a bar on the stomach, closes the throat like a gag. . . . No one has ever been able to define exactly this strange malaise.

Knocking that emanates from somewhere in our very depths, muffled, threatening knocking, like the dull throb of the blood in dilated veins, wakes us with a start. "The awakening of a condemned man" was how he used to describe those anxious startings from a troubled sleep that made him sit straight up in bed at dawn; that was how he used to speak of it, I remember, at the time when he took a certain pride in it: his delicate sensibility, his genuine disquiet. . . . "The awakening of a condemned man."

As we lie there panting for breath, we perceive little by little, the way the eye, grown accustomed to semi-darkness, begins gradually to distinguish the outlines of objects, that there is something producing this swelling, these dull twinges, a foreign body embedded in the heart of our distress like a thorn buried in the swollen flesh beneath an abscess beginning to form. It must be removed, there's no doubt about it, taken out as soon as possible, to end the malaise, the pain; we must hunt and dig, the way we probe pitilessly into the flesh with a needle to extract a splinter.

There it is, implanted in the heart of our distress, a solid corpuscle, piercing and hard, around which the pain spreads; there it is (sometimes one must grope for quite a while before finding it, at other times one comes upon it very quickly), the visual image, the idea . . . usually very simple and at first sight even somewhat childish, somewhat too naïvely crude—an image of our own death, our own life. It is this that we encounter most frequently, repressed, constricted into a limited space, like certain lives that are shown us in films or novels, presented in rigidly dramatic synopsis, heavily scored with dates (twenty years already . . . thirty . . . time gone by, youth wasted . . . finished . . . and in the end the final accounting . . .), an appallingly clear image, in which the lights and shadows are accentuated and heightened, as on a photograph reduced in size. Our lives, not the way we feel them as the days go by, like an inexhaustible fountain, constantly being replenished and scattered in impalpable, rainbow-hued drops, but hardened, petrified; a lunar landscape with its barren crests rising tragically into a desert sky, its deep craters filled with shadow.

Of course I know that he can show off and display his serenity and detachment before this credulous adolescent with an appearance of verisimilitude; it had been some time now since, in his attempts to analyze his anguish, he had last found and brought up to the surface this particular image.

Perhaps, as a result of a vague feeling that his strength had diminished, he no longer dared to attack it directly, to seize and hold on to it as he had done at one time, so that he was content to hover timidly about it, to tear off a scrap here and there, in order to cheat his sufferings; or perhaps his sensitivity had become such that almost anything, as on a delicate skin, resulted in irritation; or again, if you prefer, his distress may by now have attained such consistency that, as in a supersaturated medium, the tiniest particle produced crystallization; or perhaps he was simply suffering—as often happens with increasing age—from the sort of debilitation which I believe psychiatrists call "mind shrinkage," and enclosed as he was in a constantly narrowing circle, could only fix his attention on minute details; or was it all these together. . . ? In any case, it was no longer the general view, the wide panorama of his life and his death that made him start and tremble and kept him awake at night.

It was something minute—something so ridiculously small, so peculiar to himself, that it was hardly worth mentioning; there was really nothing to talk about, nobody could sympathize or admire, nobody could understand—a minute particle. At first he didn't notice it, he only sensed it, he became aware of its presence through a vague feeling, like the memory of a taste, or of an odor, an odor that was at once sharp and stale, and through a confused impression of dreary, grubby grayness. He recognized it, the taste and very color of fear; we both recognized it, the same taste and color as in those wan little garden plots with their clipped box shrubs, the small pebbly houses, or perhaps the surrounding woods, the rather sinister suburban woods in which macabre memories prowl among livid tree trunks and under scrubby brushwood. . . . No, this time it was a slightly sulphurous odor, the dingy grayness of the railroad station and its platform, the harrowing blowing of the train's whistle, foretelling tragic separations, wrenchings; the old woman was sitting there beside him on the bench, with her bulging stomach and her toothless mouth . . . she was looking at him out of the corner of her eye and smiling her disturbing, falsely tender smile . . . that was it, he could feel it: something which had ripened in that setting, which had burgeoned in that odor, to the sound of those whistle blasts, something solid, hard; he would have to seize it and extract it in order to soothe the swelling, the suffering . . . there it was, now he had got hold of it, it had entered into him so insidiously that at the time he had only noticed a momentary smarting, as when a thorn pierces the flesh, but now he felt it, it was the sore spot in which the twinges originated, from which the pain spread: "They aren't kind to you." Here was the judgment, the infallible verdict: "They aren't kind to you. . . ." The game was up, as well as all the flirting and teasing, evasions and shilly-shallying. There it was, ineluctable, relentless, Reality itself; he felt its sharp point buried in him like a dagger: "They aren't kind to you," and he pressed and dug and probed all around it, in the pitiless way in which one probes into swollen flesh: he knew it well, he had never had any doubt on the subject, he could die all alone like a dog, they would let him die all alone, when they no longer needed him, she especially, for she was growing more avid, more insatiable every day, she clung to him like a leech, draining off all his strength, emptying him of all substance . . . as he lay there, motionless, it seemed to him that little by little his blood was flowing from him, sucked off by her . . . he continued to press and probe, he felt something heavy, a burning lump in his chest, at the pit of his stomach, then suddenly a sharper twinge: "The fruit of forty years' hard work"—the words lacerated him like iron prongs: "Forty years of hard work," the fruit of forty years of deprivation and struggle, that was what they were devouring, that was what they were picking off bit by bit, a lot of bloodsuckers. He continued to press and to prod, there it was now, something harder, more definite still, and his distress thickened and swelled around it like foul black blood: four thousand francs, those last four thousand francs, which he had just handed out through stupidity, through sheer weariness and weakness. . . . And yet he knew them well, all those charlatans that were only after his money, the "doctor" as she called him, but she was so gullible, such a credulous, backward fool; he had even shouted "Fool!" in her face . . . with everybody else, that is; it was only with him that she was so stubborn and suspicious, other people could do what they wanted with her. With them she was as meek as a lamb, with them she was defenseless, at the mercy of the first person who came along. . . . Massage, so she needed that . . . the charlatan had probably persuaded her in no time. He could see her sticking out her neck, wagging her head: "Oh, *ee-yeess.* . . . Really, doctor? Do you think so? Do you think that would be good for me? Oh, *ee-yeess.* . . ." It was only against him that she advanced in that aggressive manner—a snake that rears its head and strikes: "Absolutely, everybody's surprised that I should have waited so long; I can hardly walk. . . ." Long walks, sports, the open

air, her latest fad, that was how she had succeeded in turning her ankle . . . but she didn't need it—he would have
liked to roll about in his bed like an angry dog that's been
stung by a wasp—she didn't even need that money, he
knew her, she had her own little pile that she had salted
away with the amounts she had dragged out of him, her
own nest egg to which she was adding at his expense . . .
only, she'd never touch it, not that, for nothing in the
world would she touch it, let him do it, her papa, he could
hear the mincing vowels . . . *paa-paa* . . . *paa-paa* . . . with
their note of stubborn, childish insistence. . . . Then, suddenly, he had a feeling of such violent rending and
wrenching—it was as though countless needles had been
stuck through his chest in every direction—that he brought
himself sharply to a sitting position: that look on her face
the other day, the way she drew back when he passed her in
the hall carrying a parcel . . . now he was like a nervous
child who, hearing a noise in the night, looks in every
corner, opens the cupboard, and then all of a sudden, as he
gropes among the clothes, thinks he feels something warm
and alive—something actually present—someone crouching there, absolutely motionless, ready to jump at him
(one doesn't dare say that he is frozen with fear, that he feels
his hair stand on end, these stereotyped images having become—often mistakenly—objects of distrust; and yet they
would express more or less literally the sensation common
to both man and child) . . . the way she jumped when he
went unexpectedly into the kitchen the other day . . . at
this point he could stand it no longer, something would
have to be done, he must act, right away, he jumped out
of bed, he must go and see, quickly, it was perhaps not yet

125

too late, perhaps after all these were only what are called night fears . . . their game of cat-and-mouse, their eternal shilly-shallying, were perhaps still permissible, just a little while longer. . . . He began to hurry, quick, no time to look for his slippers, and barefooted and in his nightshirt he raced through the hall to the kitchen and climbed on a chair to look: there it was, on the shelf above the sink—the bar of soap was there, the edge fresh cut, the very edge, sharp and well defined, of reality itself. Neither doubt nor hope was possible now; a large piece of the bar had been cut off. He looked: almost a good third. She had cut off a large piece, almost a good third. So that was why she had jumped like that, that was the meaning of her startled manner; "Oh! how you frightened me . . ." as he entered the room.

By now he had reached the very limit. He had plumbed the very depths. There was no need to look any further. After this paroxysm he felt a sort of relief. The clutched hand about his throat and chest had relaxed, he was breathing more freely as he returned to bed, carrying it with him —this concrete, hard fact—like a bone to be gnawed upon, undisturbed, in his kennel.

Back in his bed, his thought traveled about over the hard, distinct outlines, examining and feeling them, a landowner inspecting his estate: the bar of soap had been cut. She had stolen a piece of the bar of soap. He had known it all along. She had been fleecing him, sponging on him. However careful he was to leave nothing lying around, after all he couldn't lock up everything. . . . He had been right in his impression that the soap had been vanishing pretty fast lately, it was certainly not the first time. . . . Like the

126

butter last year, and the shoe polish . . . the maid had noticed it already, but there was nothing to be done about it, everything would have to be put away, she was always there, on the watch, spying around, she was nibbling things away, bit by bit, she had always deceived him, always stolen from him . . . how had she dared to cut off such a big piece, perhaps she had done it a little at a time, and yet that couldn't have been the case, she was carrying a rather large parcel. . . . Like the ball in Russian billiards which, once it has been sent on its way by a careless gesture, instead of bouncing outside the groove that confines it, runs all around the table and comes back to its starting point, his thought began to turn tirelessly round and round, with no escape possible. It circled endlessly about, coming back each time to the starting point. . . . The way she started, the way she jumped . . . the way she drew back when she passed him in the hall, it was not the first time . . . no matter how closely he watched her . . . already last year, when after goodness knows what scenes and fuss, they had finally agreed and settled upon the sum that he was to give her each month, he was convinced that she was taking butter out of his larder, it was an absolute mania with her . . . he would do better to lock things up. . . . On the other hand . . . there was the maid . . . and then he saw the whole thing again: the freshly cut bar of soap . . . her false ingenuous smile; he was right, she was fleecing him, she was picking him clean as a bone . . . he realized now that it would take him hours, he would never get to sleep, his thoughts, like the Russian billiard ball, would continue to follow the same course. Little by little it seemed to him that in his mind, as in a numbed limb, he felt a sort of cramp, a sort of heaviness, while his thought, unable to escape, kept going round and round (by this time, its path had become so well traced that from one circle to the other it underwent no change). Little by little the movement became mechanical: the way she jumped, the bar of soap, her deceitfulness, she was picking him clean, she was fleecing him. . . . He felt weary and sickened, his mind had become hardened and empty, only the little white ball kept rolling tirelessly on. He made an effort to give it a start that would send it bouncing out of the groove, he tried to push it in another direction: a book he was reading, that he had wanted to think over, a curious new theory about evolution, a very interesting book . . . however, there was nothing to be done about it, the little ball clung to its groove: the cut bar of soap, inflexible reality, held it in an unyielding grip. He turned for relief to other well-tried methods recommended in case of insomnia: he counted up to a hundred, then to a thousand, in the hope that by applying a principle similar to that used to jam a radio broadcast, he would be able to obstruct its movement, but he only succeeded in pronouncing the figures mechanically, while his imprisoned thought kept running in the same groove.

He had moments of terrible exasperation, when he felt urged to put a stop to all this at any cost, to leave his bed, hurry to his daughter's room, take her by the scruff of the neck, give her a good shaking, shout, say he had seen through her, and tell her a few home truths. But it was still dark and he was lying there helpless, she held him at her mercy, she was draining off his strength. One more sleepless night, during which she would have sucked him dry like a vampire. He would get up in the morning with his head swimming and empty.

But little by little, as dawn began to break, the little ball in his mind began to slow down. It advanced only by occasional jerks and, from time to time, even seemed about to stop. Then, when it was quite light, after the neighbors had opened their shutters, after the maid had arrived and shut the kitchen door behind her with a familiar bang— the little ball stopped altogether. A sense of calm came over him. And finally he fell off to sleep, gently, like a little child.

Waking was peaceful. The bar of soap lying on the shelf above the kitchen sink was gleaming softly in the morning sun, like iridescent sand on the beach after a night of storm.

Nothing remains of the obsessions and torments that haunt the night. They make us think of the spots and shadows that are formed on a screen, in a darkened room, by the bones of a human body when it is exposed to x-rays, and which disappear as soon as the light comes on again and the body has resumed its opacity.

For me too, the picture of that tormented, ludicrous figure hurrying along barefooted, in his nightshirt, had also faded from my memory.

And as for him, there he was again, just as though nothing had happened, looming before me the way he used to, opaque, all entrances barred. His thick contours stood out heavily against the daylight.

There was no bond between us now. No sign from him to me. Not a single glance of collusion. I might have tried to follow him, pass back and forth in front of him in order to attract his attention, to reestablish some sort of contact —he would have looked at me absent-mindedly, without seeing me.

All fear and mental anguish were forgotten.

It was extraordinary, even, to see to what extent, at the most dangerous moments of his days, he was able to remain unperturbed and calm.

He can be seen, walking with the miraculous adroitness of a lunatic, on that extreme outer edge of emptiness that occurs sometimes at the beginning of the afternoon.

Sunday afternoons, for instance, when everything seems to be wobbling in the gray air that surrounds him, pavements as well as pallid houses, he stands there firmly on his two feet (he is with friends; they are probably waiting for somebody) both hands thrust deep into the pockets of his overcoat—a compact, heavy mass, swaying silently to and fro on the edge of the pavement. He's not afraid. There he is, in the deceptive security of the little drowsy streets, right in his element. He even has a satisfied look as he stands there with his feet spread apart, swaying gently back and forth on the pavement's edge. He's playing a game. Like an enormous snake waking from sated sleep he continues to swing on one spot.

He is relaxed, at ease. He laughs with that secret laughter of his while he talks with his friends and amuses himself with cleverly aimed little digs, as though with sharp little darts, teasing them a bit, in order to feel them start up weakly, then withdraw.

On Sunday afternoons, when so many people feel a mild cramp in the solar plexus as they slip weakly into space without being able to check themselves, he walks with a firm step along the edge of fear.

When the men get together in the parlor to talk about finance and politics, as they should do, he remains aloof, listening absent-mindedly.

With his forearms resting on the arms of his chair, his rather stout thighs spread apart, leaning slightly forward, his eyes follow the younger women and girls with amused attention, as they busily pass the cakes and pour the tea. Then suddenly, when they come within his reach—the way in certain street fair games we used to try to catch hold of prizes fixed to a moving plaque, using a long pole with a ring in the end—he suddenly makes his thrust: "Hello, there. Hello. How's everything? How is everything going?" He glances at the plate of little cakes: "Nut cake, isn't it? Eh? Eh? Isn't that nut cake? Is nut cake good to eat? Do you like it? You know what it is? And how about the fandango, eh? Do you know what the fandango is? Is it a pretty dance? You know how to dance that dance, the fandango? Eh? Eh?" They blush a bit, somewhat flustered, but quickly recover their poise; they know about his strange behavior, his eccentric old-man vagaries, and they smile pleasantly, with an innocent air, trying to get out of it nicely: "Of course I know it. . . . I used to dance the fandango when I was a little girl . . . you know . . . I come from there, I was born down there. . . ." He laughs delightedly, the way he laughs for his own amusement, and tightens his hold, pulling: "Biarritz? eh? eh? Ustarritz? Do you know what that is? You know that? Ustarritz?" He rolls his r's heavily. "Biarritz? La Bidassoa? Eh? Eh? Chocoa?" or else, depending upon the individual in question: "Perros-Guirec? Eh? Eh? Ploermel? Plougastel? Pancakes? Custard pies? Eh? Pont-Aven? La Pointe du Raz?" He doesn't need to look far; anything, he knows, will do. He always picks out the timid ones, I've noticed, the refined, sensitive girls who give a start, blush more readily than the others and begin to wriggle gently, making touching efforts to free themselves: "Kotori tchass," he hurls at them, "Tchernoziom, . . . eh? eh? Novo-tcher-kassk?" He hammers out each syllable separately. ". . . No-vo-ros-siisk. . . ." He knows the easiest way to hook them; he always remembers, never makes a mistake. ". . . Kotori tchass . . . eh? eh? Vla-di-vos-tok? Pol-ta-va?" He watches with amusement while they struggle timidly, ill at ease, almost ashamed, and at the same time vaguely flattered; they smile pleasantly, anxious to please him, and reply timidly with just a shade of embarrassment: "No, I don't know Russian . . . I was born here . . . all those Russian cities . . . you know, geography was never my strongest point . . . and you, have you been there . . . ?" Smiling adorably they show their little white teeth and give a slight wriggle . . . what delightful creatures, all instinct . . . like bees or butterflies . . . that's what he frequently calls them. . . . He loves the grace of their dainty movements, their keen reflexes, that are so subtle in comparison to the argumentative ponderousness of their fathers and husbands. . . . In his delight, he gets very cocky, and prolongs the game . . . until the moment when, grown suddenly tired, he lets them go, after repeating, purely as a matter of form, almost mechanically: "Ah! really? You don't understand that? Really? You've never been there? You're not interested in geography. . . ?" in a sort of flat, weary voice. He has calmed down, he is contented. Now his gaze wanders absent-mindedly from one to the other, as he rises to go and join the men's group.

Standing there listening to them, his hands thrust in his trousers' pockets and, as usual, fingering his keys, he gravely nods his approval. Soon he enters in. He appears to be weighing his words, he seems very sure of himself: "But there's no question of it . . . there can be no question of it . . . they'll certainly not succeed. The Chamber will never allow such a project to pass . . . he'll never get a vote of confidence. . . ." Now he is arguing eagerly, quite carried away by his subject. A delightful current is set up. The men's circle, reliable and confidence-inspiring, gathers around him. Stolidly planted on his widespread feet, his hands in his pockets, clinking his keys together, he looks relaxed and sure of himself, quite in his element.

Nothing in common now, not the slightest tie between him and last night's ludicrous figure.

If, by making a great effort, I attempt to recall this tormented silhouette, it seems to me that, like my own projected shadow, it overtakes me, and again like my shadow when the sun mounts high in the sky, it rapidly diminishes, lies at my feet reduced to a small formless spot, and is reabsorbed by me.

I f it had involved her alone, I shouldn't have given it a thought. I know that she needs so little, the merest nothing makes her tremble, this Hypersensitive lined with quivering little silken tentacles that sway at the slightest breath, so that she is constantly brushed by fleeting shadows like those the gentlest of breezes can set in motion on a prairie or a wheat field.

Like dogs sniffing along a wall at suspicious odors they alone recognize, with her nose to the ground, she picks up the scent of the things people are ashamed of; she sniffs at implied meanings, follows through the traces of hidden humiliations, unable to break away from them.

Vibrating to all ugliness, she reveals their presence like a divining rod. Once, I remember, I felt as though my entire body was enveloped by a gust of hot air at the sight of her squirming because, coming out together from a theatre where I had met her with friends, I had asked them, insisting intentionally—I sensed already that she was quivering, flattened out like grass in the wind—where they lived, and offered to drive them home. I realized, if only because of her trembling, and her silent squirming beside me in the dark of the car—without ever having noticed their down-at-the-heels shoes or their threadbare overcoats, before they had even answered evasively that "it would be all right if I let them out at the corner, no need to turn, it's just a step further"—their secret humiliation which her squirming, I was sure of it, and I hated her for it, had aroused.

It was she, I knew it, who caused these feelings of shame to come out into the open and writhe under the uneasy gaze of others, she who forced the worn fingers of shabby old gloves to fold under, simply by tactfully looking away from the gloved hand in the *metro,* or people's feet to draw back under the seat. I hated her for that, and she despised me for my rude offhandedness, my blundering. In her opinion, I was not very refined, something of a boor, with neither comprehension nor friendliness, such as she had; in other words, someone who was not quite civilized. I know how extremely sensitive she is. And in fact, if she had been alone, I shouldn't have given it a thought.

I was determined, this time, that there should be nothing doing, that I would keep out of it all and observe her goings on with an air of slightly astonished incomprehension, as I had seen her do with enviable native ease to other people. I had noticed them right away; I can never help noticing them immediately. I sense them, really, almost before I see them. I can never help perceiving the slightest electric shock that comes from her, nor can I help vibrating in unison when it occurs. It's because of that, too, that I have often really hated her, because of the sort of complicity, the humiliating promiscuity that, in spite of myself, exists between us, the sort of fascination she has for me which forces me to follow in her tracks, head down, sniffing foul odors, the way she herself does.

It was at their house, at a luncheon to which I had been invited, I've forgotten on what occasion, it's already quite a while ago. I had seen immediately (she is never entirely outside my field of vision, even when I seem to be absent-minded, or busy looking elsewhere), I had noticed her eyes right away, the way they suddenly began to scurry about like a magnetic needle that starts oscillating more rapidly from one side of the electrometer to the other, indicating an increase of current. The corners of her mouth were slightly contracted, as though from a nervous twitch. I felt that she wanted to make a stand about something, to intervene in order to keep something from happening, to stop it from happening, but that all she could do was to squirm in one spot in that silent, hardly perceptible way of hers.

But I was determined, that day, to go my own way, to remain aloof. And in order to accentuate my disapproval, my remoteness, I assumed the indifferent, calm gaze of a thick-skinned sybarite, which at times she finds so irritating; a gaze that visibly had concluded, after taking stock, that there was nothing that might justify all this ridiculous grimacing, nothing worth mentioning—and, in reality, there was nothing, or so I tried to persuade myself—nothing except what the other guests doubtless could see as well as I, that is to say, the atmosphere of rather forced cordiality, the tension and slight discomfiture generally experienced at the beginning of a meal shared by companions who are not very well suited to one another or have little in common. I was prepared, whatever she should do, to take things easy with the other guests, in their habitually happy state of innocent, complacent unawareness. And even, in order to emphasize the distance between her and me, and to break off all contact, I felt rather in the mood, should an opportunity present itself, to perpetrate a real howler, as I do sometimes when she exasperates me too much, to deliberately "put my foot in it," as she probably says furiously.

However, it was impossible for me, despite my repugnance, despite my laziness, not to notice this time, that others, among those present, were behaving in a manner similar to hers, revealing a sort of vague apprehension and excitement, a silent uneasiness such as animals have before an approaching storm.

There were moments when the old servant who was passing the platter seemed to be bending over a little lower than usual, and she too, like grass in the wind, was wearing a look of apprehension and expectation. There was something about her, with her eyes lowered and her attention apparently fixed only on presenting the platter steadily on her upturned palm, something that retracted and tautened, that was at once both frightened and avid.

As for the old man, when, after forcing myself to make

the effort, I finally decided to look at him, hoping still that I was mistaken, I saw that his hail-fellow manner and gruff, rough-diamond cordiality had disappeared: he was silent, frowning, tapping nervously on the table.

That was all that was needed, my vague impulses towards independence and innocence were over and done with. I immediately slipped back into my role of conducting rod through which all the currents that charged the atmosphere were passing.

Now the conversation had a different sound for me; it had lost its apparently banal, harmless aspect, and I sensed that certain words that were being spoken gave on to vast craters, immense precipices, visible only to initiates, who were leaning, restraining themselves. . . . I was leaning with them, restraining myself, trembling and attracted as they were—over the abyss.

But as we sat there all huddled up, listening, we reminded one rather of the members of an audience, staring in the air with hunched shoulders, looking at the performance of a tightrope walker, or of an acrobat about to leap, or watching, with bated breath, as a sleepwalker advances sure-footedly on the very edge of a roof, along the cornice.

Dieppe—they were talking about Dieppe and the nearby country, about Pourville where, it just so happened, that all of them, one year or another, had spent the summer: the pebbly beaches are ugly, said one young guest, he was doing most of the talking, but the sea . . . nowhere are its shadings so beautiful and so varied . . . there is one particularly charming spot, the golf links, the one between Pourville and Dieppe, which is more beautifully situated than any he had ever seen—the young acrobat was advancing nimbly on the tightrope and we were watching him—unless it be the Gairloch links, in Scotland, up in the magnificent lake district. He adored that, he said, and we continued to watch him: he was swinging nonchalantly back and forth now, hanging by his hands in space . . . he loved to play golf on links that were right on a cliff like that, where the sea breeze and the briny air blended with the delicious smell of trampled grass . . . he swung back and forth while we kept on watching him . . . at any moment now, he was about to take off—"Do you play golf," he asked, "have you ever played?" She nodded her head feebly by way of a no: "No, no . . ." she had never played . . . she didn't play . . .—"You should . . ." he was swinging very fast, he was about to leap: "And how about you, sir," he turned towards the old man, "it's a sport that has the advantage of being suitable to all ages, it's never too late . . . the English . . ." the unwitting, innocent young fool was on the point of crashing down at our feet, a formless, limp rag, lying in the dust. . . . Yet, no, nothing happened . . . and we heard the old man reply in a voice in which only we could detect the rather forced shading, the slightly hoarse note that revealed the reality of the danger that had threatened: "No, but even so I think it's a bit late to start, I'm too old, and the fact is, to tell the truth, I'm not like your English friends. . . ." Everything was going fine. The young acrobat had brilliantly caught hold of the other trapeze, with the greatest of ease. But suddenly he started swinging again, in order to take the leap . . . one minute more and again, from a greater distance, this time, and from higher up, he took it: "But how about you," he said, turning to her, "you would love that, I'm certain, there's nothing like a good morning walk, on grass that is still

140

dewy . . . how free, one feels so free, so light and airy, alone, because—and that's one of the great advantages of this delightful sport—if you want, you can do without a partner. The caddie follows at a short distance . . . a caddie is absolutely necessary . . . nothing so spoils one's pleasure as having to tote one's own clubs. . . ." The prison doors had swung open and light was streaming in . . . he was not a young acrobat doing the high jump, but Saint George, sparkling with audacity and purity, advancing towards her, sword in hand, in order to deliver her . . . but she clung to the wall, in the darkest corner, her head turned away . . . she did not want to look, she knew that she must not look, nor rise and go towards him, into the pure air and the light, towards fearless deeds, towards offhanded, carefree deeds . . . all huddled together, clinging to the wall just as she was, with heads lowered, we were waiting . . . he went straight ahead: "Don't you agree, sir, that your daughter should take up golf? I shall be her teacher, if you come anywhere near us this summer, my parents have a country place there. . . ." The dragon did not budge, but sat there motionless, a bogus, bland smile on its half-open jaws: "Why, certainly, why certainly. . . . Why not? Why not, indeed. . . ." The door was open, they had only to go out, what were they waiting for? Who was holding them back? But she did not want to risk it, she refused, her eyes were scurrying from side to side, her voice came pale and affected, choked: "Oh! thank you, you're very kind, but I really don't believe, I don't believe that I should ever have the patience, I should never be able to do it, I'm a bit too old. . . ." The old man looked at her, she felt, we all felt, how much he hated her at that moment, how he despised us, how ashamed he was for us, disgusted even, as he saw us

141

all there cowering ignominiously, flattened against the wall, bent over, biting the dust.

He was about to leap at us, or else hurl himself at the young fool in order to crush him, trample on him and reduce him savagely to a pulp, as he so well knows how to do. . . . When no, once again, a miracle had occurred . . . he suddenly turned away from her and from us, leaving us to our state of abjection. Innocence, purity, lightheartedness had won the day. . . . He was bound in their direction, won over, he took his place on their side.

With the air of admiring, fond indulgence of the faithful old servants, the old butlers in English plays who smilingly regard the pranks of the master's sons whom they've known as children, and whose fathers they have watched grow up, he smiled at his young friend: "Well, and how about me? You don't think I'm too old to start? Because I haven't said no, after all. You tempt me. No, I haven't said no. My doctor would be in favor of it, since he has advised me to walk a lot. And the sticks, how do you call them, the clubs. . . ? They have very complicated names . . . How do you pronounce it? Eh? The mashie? the mashie? and the niblick? ho-ho, the ni-blick?" He laughed his hearty laughter. Relaxed and at ease, we laughed with him.

The explosion, the eruption we had been waiting for, all huddled up together, the frightening tidal-wave of cinders, burning ashes and boiling lava, had not taken place. Nothing had happened—hardly a few crevices, a fine thread of evanescent smoke revealing to the trained eye that the volcano was in action.

Once again, I had been all worked up, and for nothing at all.

142

*P*rudence. They are very prudent. Indeed they never take any very great risks. One has to spy on them for a long time before one is aware of their slight quivering, their treadmill motions, like the ebb and flow of a tideless sea that hardly comes in or goes out at all, with little lapping waves.

Nor do they ever put themselves forward very much. You have to lie in wait a long time, and keep hidden watch, before you see them move. Many people in my place, I realize, would get exasperated at this game, and become discouraged. But not me, I'm going to be patient. I'm going to resist the temptation that seizes me frequently, when I see them so inert, to hit them, to give them just one little blow that would push them a bit, and force them to get out of that stagnant water in which they stretch themselves calmly with weak, flabby motions, and bring them forth into broad daylight, up to the surface, where people move freely with broad, precise gestures, by immense, exciting leaps and bounds.

But I know what would happen if I were to take that liberty. I know them. They would change right away. All at once, they would solidify and become hard and strong. Imposing. Arrogant. Absolutely unapproachable. They would get on their high horse with me and keep me at a distance—strangers who wouldn't let me come near them. That secret bond, known only to ourselves, that attraction we feel, would be all over between them and me. No longer would we experience, they and I, those mysterious tensions that exist between us, those vibrations that resemble the vibrations a tuning fork receives from the object it strikes.

For me, they would become nothing more than big, jointed dolls, made for others, by others, and with which I didn't know how to play.

Therefore, I must continue. I've already said this, I believe, but I have never been in a position to choose. I must have patience. Keep watching. See them relax weakly, with hardly perceptible movements—those of an amoeba on its glass slide—then pull themselves together again almost immediately.

How prudent he is. And how safe he keeps. It's not easy to take him unawares. He never ventures outside the norm other than with little frightened jumps, then runs right back to safety.

And at that, more often than not, it was the others who provoked and drew him out.

I have asked myself more than once what might be the mysterious attraction that he has for them, even at a distance, the irresistible need that forces them to "seek him out," as we say, to go rub up against him from time to time, at their own risk.

Motionless, like a great spider in its web, he seems to know that he doesn't need to budge, that he has only to wait for them. Nor will they fail to come, attracted as they are, like flies.

The old servant, seated at her work table in the little back room looking out on the dark courtyard, during the overquiet early afternoon hours, when time seems to withdraw into itself to watch and to wait, felt as though she had "pins and needles" in her soul: she sensed a sort of cramp, a numbness that would have to be shaken off. Or perhaps she felt vaguely, at the very heart of her torpor, the stifled urge of some sort of heavy, dubious sensuality.

But she doesn't admit that, of course. There are things to which they never give freedom of the city, things they never deign to take into consideration, those little eddies within themselves, those little waves that keep following one another without stopping: how could we live, in fact, if we had to stop and take note of all that, pass our time splitting hairs and looking for complications where none exists . . . ? No, she wouldn't even think about it, she would tell you in all good faith that she would rather get her work done. . . . there's so much of it . . . in this house it's never all done, there's work enough for two. . . . But she just remembered that she must show Monsieur, he being so finicky about such things. . . . Oh, he insists on things being in order all right, rather close-fisted, too, like lots of people at that age especially, and I'll say he's a real crank, however he may look as though he's in the clouds, as regards anything that belongs to him . . . I must show him . . . it's a regular flood . . . the paper's ruined . . . the curtain is all discolored . . . I must take advantage of his being alone now . . . sitting there in his study doing nothing . . . he must come and see. . . . That's always their method, I've already said so, the way they always need an alibi. The way, when they timidly risk sticking their noses out of their own hole, they have to take down from the wall an outfit of some sort, one of the various types of armor they wear —there are always some on hand, ready for their use, more than they know what to do with—then advance prudently, under its protection: What's the matter? I don't understand . . . I haven't got time. . . . The days here aren't long enough . . . I must go tell him. . . . It would be a loss of time to try a direct attack on her, against that hard smooth surface of hers.

Bent over double, she pattered down the hall. There was a funny look on her face, an air about her that reminded one rather curiously of the conventional stage procuress: obsequious, enticing and slightly fluttery. She realized, apparently, that this was a dish seasoned to his taste, that what she was about to hand him was a treat of his own choosing; something, she probably sensed it vaguely, that he himself had planted in her and that now, as he sat there, he had caused to germinate, to burgeon in her. . . . Both he and his daughter, I've noticed that, have a rather special gift of making people do certain things, or say certain words: it's as though they possessed little invisible harpoons that catch hold of people, or magnets that lift and attract them. With her, it's especially when she is embarrassed or afraid, or when she's lying in ambush, all aquiver, that, to the great astonishment of everybody, even from the mouths of babes and sucklings, there come words that go straight to her and cling to her most sensitive spots like flies to flypaper.

With him, it's slightly different. When he sits quite still, huddled up to himself, without knowing what makes them do it, people rise and go to him. Dogs. "A dog that brings a bone"—that's what I call them when they arrive, cringing, then come servilely a little nearer, holding in their teeth what he himself has thrown to them, lay it at his feet and wait with a begging look, for something they themselves don't know quite what, a pat of approval, or a kick.

She knocked softly, her voice the unctuous voice of the devoted servant: "Am I disturbing you, sir? It's about the faucet that must not have been properly turned off . . . it's so hard to turn . . . and the wall is all wet. . . . You ought to see what the paper looks like. . . ."

You're never sure with him, you're never sure to win. He didn't seem to like very much the dish she had just handed him. His lip curled (in a sort of pout that she knew well), he closed his book grumbling, there's never any peace . . . they're always waiting behind doors, ready to enter at the slightest sign of weakening. This time he was a bit sleepy, on the point of taking a little snooze. She had seemed almost to sense that—she had come running right away, taking advantage of his weakness. She stood there waiting, staring at him with her motionless, round, bird's eyes. She knew perfectly well that she was trying to drag him down to her level—they're much slyer, much less unaware, in reality, than people think, despite their look of stupid, harmless poultry: being jealous (they are jealous of such things as that), she was delighted to have him to herself, outside the world he lived in where, as she probably sensed, vaguely he moved high above her, he escaped her—in order to imprison him in her own world, the one she lived in, which was both hard and harsh, rugged of surface, threatening. . . . Certainly she enjoyed that, to be able to drag him there, to that hole, to that oozing spot, into that squalor which she thought belonged to both of them, but which belonged only to her. . . . He didn't want to have anything to do with it. . . .

But neither did he put up any resistance. She could be sure of one thing: he would never send her away. Never would he dare break up the complicity that had existed between them for years. Pushing his chair back, he rose: "All right, all right, I'll go look at it."

One of my favorite ideas is that most assassinations only take place with the assent—unconscious, naturally—of the victim.

She had not been mistaken, she had been sure, as she went there attracted by him without knowing very well how, to rub up against him and let him stroke her back, that she was bringing him what really suited him, even though he hadn't wanted to recognize that fact and had appeared so disgusted—this was the fodder he had been waiting for.

In the early afternoon, as I said before, there are dangerous moments. Not for everybody, of course. Most people —and I am not speaking only of very busy people who are always peculiarly well protected against such dangers as these—most people pass lightly through these moments the way well-trained mountain climbers leap over crevices without looking underfoot.

This is the hour given over to the "siesta," to rest; the moment, after the excitement of the midday meal, when those who stay behind alone in the silent rooms, suddenly experience a sensation of cold; their heart in their mouth, they are seized with a dizziness, an impression that the earth has suddenly fallen out from under their feet and that they are slipping, without being able to restrain themselves, into the void.

This is probably a comparable illusion, in reverse, to the one we have when, in a moving train, the telegraph poles seem to be moving too. This impression of falling and dizziness that people have comes perhaps from the fact that they feel, in this silence, before this void, the cold, anonymous touch of time, the ceaseless dropping away of the seconds whose passing they suddenly become aware of, the way, when blood leaves the face, freckles that had passed unnoticed under a rosy complexion become visible and stand out under pallor.

There's nothing around them that they can clutch at, nothing around them except an immense gray stretch along which they feel themselves slipping as down a smooth wall —and feeling about here and there, they look for something, a rough spot, some sort of hold, something hard and dependable, to which they can cling.

Then it is that they see them appear: they watch them become slowly visible, at a distance, heartening, promising and alluring, like a mirage in the arid wastes of the desert.

Delightfully presented, scattered about in the velvet-draped shop windows, they shine through the highly polished panes, like cool pebbles gleaming under the shimmering clearness of a stream. . . . Things . . . things whose sharply cut outlines, whose finished, perfect outlines enclose a dense, firm substance: cigar holders, watches, handbags, fine leather billcases, bottles, lighters, valises. . . . Immediately this thought, like a blindworm around a proffered stick, winds itself tightly around them.

That heartinthemouth, that sensation of dizziness, disappear all of a sudden. The Rubicon is passed.

Once again they feel that they are on firm ground, that they are saved, as they go out into the bright light of the early afternoon, and turn towards the sparkling shop-windows and busy streets, borne along by the delightful presentiment of a calming, joyful effort to be made, of a delicately skillful feat to be accomplished, of all the possible luck and the possible risks, by the delightful excitement of adventure.

Between them and a formless, strange, threatening universe, the world of things has interposed itself like a screen, to protect them.

Behind it, no matter where, they feel safe. This is the

quilted casket, silky and warm, in which they betake themselves from one end of the world to the other: Venice . . . things made of tortoise shell . . . frames of lapis lazuli . . . that honey-colored cigarette holder gleaming in the lighted window on the corner of a dark, squalid little street: their avid eyes had caught it right away that day as they were coming home worn out from an exhausting visit to churches and museums, emerging, somewhat bewildered, from an austere, coldly distant universe . . . London with its gloves, its billcases that are even more flexible, and wear longer than those from Berlin . . . Dresden tea sets . . . Moscow with its cashmere shawls . . . that fine linen tablecloth with cross-stitch embroidery, that lasts forever, after fifteen years it's like new . . . Constantinople . . . carpets . . . Madrid . . . silk shawls . . . Fez and its embroidered leather slippers. . . .

They may be seen, as similar to highly priced merchandise as possible, or to brand new dolls, in their well-ironed clothes, and their glass eyes set in their inanimate faces; they may be seen seated in hotel lobbies or on tearoom terraces, staring with a curious intensity at the people who pass by, pruning and trimming with their sharp eyes, as though with shears, whatever is showy, formless, naïvely ridiculous, carefree, happy-to-be-alive, awkward or casual: those ankles are too thick, that bosom too ample, that hat —the poor woman seems to have taken the lamp shade by mistake—that coat—it must have been made out of a portiere—lopping off with quick little whacks all imperfections and flaws, all that, either through weakness, slackness, unpardonable negligence, or insufferable off-

151

handedness, diverges from the norm, transgresses the relentless, subtle, sure rules, the secret of which they possess.

Conventional, worn-out old metaphors come to mind, despite oneself, "the pact with the devil," or the famous broomstick of the "sorcerer's apprentice," when we see them, snugly enclosed in their quilted caskets, paying each day a heavier tribute for their eternally threatened security.

Their fanatical eye never abandons its uneasy, ferret's vigil in order to discover in the smooth, impervious protecting wall, some defect, the tiniest of cracks. . . .

Like ants working tirelessly in an effort to rebuild an ant-hill that is crumbling on every side, like women who are continually refreshing their delicate make-up, they scurry about, filling in holes, adding new plaster . . . like varnish the construction that surrounds them is constantly cracking and peeling . . . and through the tiny fissure, an undefinable threat, something relentless and intolerable that exists on the other side, always ready to worm its way in, keeps seeping through, stealthily. . . . Under its pressure the peeling and abrasion grow inordinately; it advances upon them, filling their entire field of vision the way close-ups cover the whole screen in a film. And all their contained anguish, suddenly liberated, aroused as by a draught of air, swells and tautens towards this abyss. . . .

Lonely men, women whom "life," as they say, has already treated rather badly, widows, their children dead, one of scarlet fever—"You should have seen what a darling he was . . . Why? he used to ask—he could say extraordinary

152

things, he was so cute—why must we love people since one day we shall have to be separated from them? . . . he had blond curls, if you curled them around a stick in the morning they stayed curled all day . . . what a waste, I always said, such lovely hair on a boy"—women with faded eyes and worn-out bodies get up at daybreak—they must hurry to go and see . . . that hole is still there . . . that spot . . . and yet they had rubbed it hard . . . yesterday, in the light, even if you looked at it very closely, you might have thought that it had disappeared for good . . . and yet, there it is, you can see it two yards off, threatening, hostile, mocking them right in the middle of the parlor, with a reddish ring around it . . . it's still there, on the shelf, you can't see anything else, it "knocks your eyes out," it destroys the soothing unity of that smooth, gold row of Saint-Simon's complete works, there in the place of the mislaid volume—is something disquieting, intolerable, a dark, empty space, a hole. . . .

There it was, in the wall . . . a regular flood . . . the wall was wet through. . . . Readjusting his glasses with impatient fingers, he leaned over, knelt down, his cheek against the tiled floor, in order to see better. . . . Naturally, he saw it perfectly well, there, right at the bottom of the wall, under the bathtub, there where the damp plaster had begun to peel . . . an oozing, greenish spot, a crack. . . . All at once he felt something clutch hold of him, grip him tight, and, clenching him as though with a slipknot, begin to pull.

Sitting in the usual spot in his study, behind the half-closed shutters that protected him from the glaring light of

153

the early summer afternoon, he felt himself become enveloped little by little, as though by a sheet of thick liquid, by the oppressive calm, the silence.

The motions of his mind as, fidgeting impatiently in his chair, he read one of his favorite books, at the same time that he made every effort, from out of his torpor, to catch hold of something resistant and hard and press it, as he is able to do with such ease in his good moments, the motions of his mind resembled the uncertain, slack motions of a deep-sea diver trying to pick up an object on the bottom of the ocean. Despite the obstinacy of his awkward efforts, he succeeded in grasping nothing but a flabby, inert substance that crumbled at his touch.

Even the very solid matter which he considered to be presented in its most concentrated form in textbooks for twelve-year-olds, that smooth, hard rattle that was usually so soothing to his irritated gums, this time when he made an effort to triturate it, he had the impression that it had collapsed, that it was lying flat and limp—an empty envelope.

And as his mind grew tense, the way a muscle does, without encountering any resistance, he felt more and more a sort of painful cramp, like the cramp we should feel in our jaws if we were to chew liquid food for a long time, or perhaps the exasperation one might feel at the realization that one has lifted an empty weight, with an arm that was tense and ready for effort, or, shall we say, the irritation we sometimes feel when we do Swedish gymnastics, arms up, arms down, knees bent, knees straight, stoop down, stand up, on the balls of our feet. . . .

It seemed to him that the force which he projected

towards the outside world, being incapable of self-absorption, had gathered within him little by little, like water in the legs and arms of a dropsical patient. Vaguely, somewhere inside him, he felt it weighing on him, pressing and contracting, with twinges of dull shooting-pains.

These are the moments, I've noticed, when, in order to calm this irritation, finding nothing outside himself, and reduced to his own resources, in order to extract from himself something tangible and alive, his most genuine, most intimate essence, in a gesture that is peculiar to him, he rubs the knuckle of his folded thumb hard against his gums, at the root of his teeth, then holds it under his nose and sniffs. This soothes and at the same time exasperates him, his own secret, sweetish, slightly sickening smell.

It was at this very psychological moment that the servant, warned by goodness knows what, came to present him with the leak under the bathtub, the crack, the spot. . . .

The relief he felt, in spite of his disgruntled manner, was probably similar to that experienced by a neurasthenic lying prostrate on his bed for years, when he hears an alarm bell ring in the nursing home. . . . She had taken hold of him by the collar and dragged him out of the debilitating torpor in which he had been soaking—outside, into broad daylight, he had felt that he was once again on firm ground, he was saved already, as he started running: "Where'd you say it was? Where's that? In the bathroom? But I've said a hundred times that the faucet should be turned off tight. . . . And you say there's a hole in the wall? In the wall?" There it was finally, the hard, sure obstacle . . . his relieved thoughts seized upon it and held it with avidity. Here it was, seasoned exactly to his taste—she knows them well, her intuitions, like those of any old faithful servant, may be relied upon—the oozing, green spot, a hole through which soapy water was leaking . . . the crack in the wall . . . it must have been seeping through for a long time without anybody having mentioned it. . . . He clutched hold of it now, with all his might. . . . *Tstt* . . . *Tstt* . . . with an impatient gesture he brushed aside the servant who, eagerly, and with a sort of satisfied pride at the results obtained, began to explain: "It's probably a leak in the supply main that runs behind the wall, it finally burst. . . ." *Tstt* . . . *tstt* . . . he brushed her aside, she should keep quiet. . . . It was not in the supply main, certainly not, it was there . . . he knelt down, lay down, his cheek against the tile floor . . . it was there, in the pipe, the water was seeping through, it was leaking all down the wall . . . he was on all fours, his upturned buttocks stretched his trousers to the splitting point . . . the servant would have liked to laugh, but she knew that this was no time for joking, this would be a pretty time to laugh, it was all right for other people to take a refined, detached attitude—he lay flat on the floor, stretched out his arm, it was quite a leak, it had gone clean through the wall, to the other side, surely, he pushed her aside and ran to look at the other side as well, no doubt about it, the water was seeping through, the paper was all gray, it had come unpasted and was hanging down; as for the curtain . . . the curtain . . . he lifted it up and felt it with impatient clumsy fingers, readjusted his glasses and looked at it closely, his lip curled in an expression he always wore at such moments—he made a strange face, full of hatred, shame and loathing—while she, there beside him, shook her head with the calm air of a connoisseur: "Oh!

it's entirely spoiled now, I don't think anything can be done about it . . . with reps like that it'll be hard to make it look like anything again." He looked at her with a haggard expression and repeated mechanically: "Hard to make it look like anything? Hard to make it look like anything?"

He had been torn from the malleable cozy world in which he dwelt so snugly, and roughly projected into the hard, aggressive, relentless world that was hers, over which he had no hold. He turned towards her, looking for support: "How do you mean? How do you mean it'll be hard to make it look like anything again?" He had plunged, head downward, into that hostile world in which he felt himself an outsider, threatened from every side: "And what about dyeing it? What if it was sent to be dyed . . ." he was making a great effort: "What if the curtain was entirely redyed?" She hesitated. . . . "Perhaps . . . it would have to be shown to the cleaner. . . . But then. . . ." She was smiling a funny, slightly mocking smile in which, at the same time, could be seen a sort of fed-up apprehension, and made a bantering gesture with her hand: "Certainly, but . . . the price . . . that. . . ." Only now did the pocket inside him, which had swollen like water under the skin of a dropsical patient, burst entirely . . . the pain he felt was so great that it outweighed all feeling of relief. . . . "Of course . . . But that didn't just start up. . . ." He was raging. ". . . that didn't just start up today. It took longer than a half hour for it to get like that . . . nobody had told him anything, it had been kept from him . . . the crack, the hole in the wall . . . the plumber had already explained it the last time . . . in this house, he has to be called in every

157

other day . . . that hole didn't get there all by itself . . . it wasn't in the supply main . . . that wasn't true. . . ." He was shouting, while the servant drew back, frightened. ". . . you know that's not true, about the faucet that's never turned off right . . . all night long, I can hear the shower dripping . . . I have to get up in the middle of the night to turn it off after them . . . with their baths and ablutions . . . English style . . . cold showers . . . all their absurd theories about hygiene . . . their mania for cleanliness . . . that habit they have—but I'll break them of it—of soaking themselves for hours, stretched out there like logs. . . ."

While he was shouting, the pocket was emptying. The pain, although still quite sharp, was mitigated by a sort of enjoyment, especially since, at that very moment, they were certainly there, shut up in their rooms, reading, or lying on their beds in an attitude that he felt was peculiarly offhanded and provocative, forever rereading, with rapturous admiration, the works of their favorite poets, written especially for snobs and failures. It was then that his own pleasure began, when he could pull them from their beds, snatch the book from their hands, throw it to the other end of the room and, dragging them still bewildered from their refuge, lead them to the spot, to the curtain, grab them tight by the scruff of the neck, force them to their knees and rub their noses in it. He fumed about for a long time, then, when the pocket was quite drained and he had finally let them go—relaxation set in.

He felt all weak and sore, as though he had just been through a drunken spree. He needed gentleness and help. The shouting and the raging had only served to conceal

158

from him for a moment the spot and the faded curtain. But they were still there before his eyes, sordid and sad, like the little paper balls and the soiled paper streamers that lie around at dawn on the benches and floor of a hall in which people have danced all night.

He turned towards the servant, seeking consolation and sympathy. He had a touching air about him, somewhat uneasy, like a contrite child. He was alone, unable to cope with all that, as she well knew. . . . "So then . . . did she really think that if she took it to the cleaner. . . ? The price. . . ." Frowning, he pulled himself together with a final effort . . . his voice was weak and hoarse. ". . . the price . . . but what's to be done about it . . . ? Enough damage had been done already. . . . And how about the paper?" He would have liked to let himself be coddled, like a child. ". . . the paper? Did she really think they could find a matching roll? But what about the color. . . . ? He didn't know . . . he knew nothing about such things . . . the paper in the parlor must be faded . . . they would have to look at it by daylight. . . . Was she sure? Did she think the color of the paper hadn't changed?" He felt weak, drained of his strength, all he wanted was to be reassured: "Really not? It doesn't show too much? And did she think she could find it? With exactly the same grain? Because it just happened to be right in the parlor, in full view. . . ." Not at all, she would fix it, she would be able to match it, nobody would see a thing, nobody would notice, especially if the curtain weren't drawn, the exact spot where the two sorts of paper, the old and the new, were to be joined together—the hole would be stopped up, the paper would be pasted on the wall . . . the threat would be averted

159

. . . he wouldn't be able to see the crack anymore, the crack through which something relentless and intolerable had seized hold of him by main force and was dragging him along, through which his very life, it seemed to him, was ebbing away. . . .

Once more, everything was going to turn out all right.

Relieved and soothed he was now able to trot somewhat embarrassed, back to his study, resume his seat in the middle of the universe he had woven for himself, start it swinging, according to his mood, with renewed satisfaction and vigor, watch it come to life under his gaze and assume color again, fresh and iridescent as a sparkling spider web on which, after the rain, little rain-bow-hued drops, clinging to the silken threads, tremble and gleam in the sun.

And yet it would be the natural thing, it would be the normal thing." She felt like writhing and stamping with rage and impatience: everybody understood that, everybody said it to her. Even the doctor, the last time she had gone to consult him, had been surprised: "And yet it would be the natural thing"—he had said that to her—"and yet it would be the normal thing. Strange, that your father shouldn't understand. . . . Somebody absolutely must speak to him." With an energetic gesture he had passed the blotter over the prescription he had just written out. "It's really one of the rare cases for which medicine can perform wonders. It would be a pity not to take advantage of that fact." He had had the self-assured, indifferent tone, that they always have when they make their oracular statements that give such an irrefutable, impressive air to what they say.

She felt like stamping her feet like a spoiled child who has been refused the toy he wants somebody to buy for him, which he considers his right. It was her right. Everybody told her so. Even the doctor had been surprised. Everybody understood that: he was her father. There was no use trying to wriggle out of it: she was his daughter. However often he refused, however much he fumed, nothing would change that: he was her papa. That was the norm, the law with which she would force him to comply. It wouldn't help for him to turn away sullenly, with an air of being fed up, she would find a way to force him. . . .

It was this certainty, this conviction she had of enforcing the rules, of carrying out the orders of an infallible power, to which both of them must submit, that gave her, when she appeared tight-lipped in the doorway, that inexorable, obstinate, opinionated look, as though she were ready to brave anything, all sorts of whims and scenes, the look that trained nurses have when they arrive at the appointed hour in the room of a "difficult" patient, a poultice or a syringe in their hands. . . .

And yet I know well, it must never be forgotten—nothing is ever quite simple with them, I know exactly what they're like, always double-faced, not to say triple- or many-faced, evasive and full of all kinds of little secret recesses. . . . There was something else, too, that impelled her to rise suddenly with the air of a clairvoyant guided by strange voices, and go to him, sweeping aside all obstacles. A call that came from him. An obscure, strange attraction. Something that she feels moving inside her, when she sits there curled up on the foot of her bed, in the calm and the propitious torpor of the summer afternoons, a coiled snake that starts gently to uncoil and lifts its head. It's for that reason, I have always suspected, always known, too, it's for that reason, because she feels, coiled up inside her, this strange need, this attraction, that she goes around asking everybody, she needs to be advised, to be reassured, she doesn't know, is it natural, normal at her age, ah! *ee-ee-yes?* Really? for her to need him as she does, because it's hard, isn't it, it's hard for a woman alone, and he's all she has left in the world, now that her poor mother is dead. . . . That's why she stands there in that imploring way of hers, hands crossed on her stomach, masquerading, all in mourning, her lisle-thread gloves and her black cotton stockings. . . . The placid-faced old women—the same ones with whom I, too, in my moments of dejection, had tried to curry favor, but in vain, they're suspicious of me, I don't inspire confidence in them—these old women, at sight of her, felt sorry for her, shook their heads. . . . "Certainly, poor soul. And when you think that she's all he's got in the world. Really, some people don't deserve to have children. There's one good thing, however, he can't take it with him. . . . She's quite right. She'd be wrong to feel uncomfortable. She's his daughter, isn't she? And no matter what he does, he can't get away from that. . . ." They give a careful coating, a wrapping to what she has so cleverly furnished them, the strange need, the obscure, dubious attraction (but of course they don't see it that way, these are things

163

that, in their simplicity, in their great purity, they never see, and they act without realizing what they're doing, impelled by an unconscious instinct); they place it in a strong container—such as they always keep on hand—all prepared, all addressed and packed with every precaution, well protected—in which, like an explosive enclosed in its thick, powerful armature, she can convey it in all security to him as he sits back there, waiting—a motionless target, to be aimed at.

As for him, he knew when she arrived that she was not alone. They were always there, right behind her, he knew it, that army of female dispensers, her protectresses, whom she had sought out and who never refuse her their support. Their silent, drab multitude was there backing her, urging her on. When she appeared in the doorway, with her stiff expression, her bulging eyes staring straight before her, their inexpressive faces pressed forward behind her, like the smooth, waxlike features of the saints who surround the set figures of the Virgin in primitive paintings.

He had known them for a long time. Already, years ago, it was they he had felt watching him, the first time, as he had leaned over the cradle, somewhat moved, uneasy, adjusting his glasses on his nose in order to see more clearly, when he had heard her aggressive, stubborn cry (the sensation was still fresh, unexpected)—they were all there then, around the cradle, wagging their heads with a serious satisfied air, like the wicked godmothers in fairy tales.

It was they, the first day, who had brought her to him—a bundle swathed in covers—and had laid her in his arms with a triumphant, slightly mocking air. They had tickled the bundle, making their thick, flabby fingers run up and down it, water-soaked fingers, with broad, spatulate nails, nurses' and midwives' fingers, with clever, prehensile movements, and they had simpered, sticking out their lips in a gluttonous gesture: "Just look at that now, isn't it cute; now, isn't it sweet, look how proud it is already to be held in its papa's arms. . . . Yes ma'am, that's my papa, that's my papa, all right. . . ." They hugged the bundle to them, they swung it towards him to tease him, their lips puckered in a voluptuous, gluttonous pout: "That's my papa, all right. . . . How proud and happy my papa is to have such a fine little girl, such a fine little girl"—they stuck out their lips with a relish,—"yes, ma'am. . . ." Already, even then, as he had held out his arm awkwardly to take her—"No, no, not that way, oh! what an awkward thing a papa is, that hurts, doesn't it, my lambkin, my precious, its papa doesn't know how to hold it right. . . ." As he had put out his arm obediently, his elbow bent, he had felt his face grow inert and heavy, set, in spite of himself; it had seemed to him that invisible threads, glued to him, were drawing him along, or that a sticky coating spread all over him was hardening and adhering to him like a mask.

He must have felt already, while they were chattering and simpering and swinging the bundle smilingly in his direction, that this bundle in their hands was an instrument, like a sounding tube with which they were trying gently to probe him, which they were inserting into him delicately, with the help of their vaselined voices, a drain through which a part of himself, his very substance, would trickle away.

Or perhaps it seemed to him rather, as he felt her close to him, warm and spineless and already avid—an insatiable, obstinate little animal—that she was like a leech applied to him in order to bleed and weaken him.

Nor had she ever consented to abandon the position in which her fairy godmothers had laid her, huddled up against him, battening on his substance, drinking his blood.

On the contrary, little by little she had perfected her knowledge of his soft spots, his sensitive points. And it was in these spots, at these points, that she preferred to curl up, that she caused to gather and ooze forth something that, without her, he knew, would have remained diffused and diluted within him; but she clung to him like a damp, hot compress that draws pus up to the skin and causes an abscess to ripen.

When she was still just a child, on Sunday afternoons, at the silent but inexorable injunction of the "fairies," he would "take her walking." The entire neighborhood, in fact, seemed to exert upon him the same heavy, mute compulsion that forced him to stroll slowly along, holding her by the hand, amidst the crowds in their Sunday best, on the dreary avenue, bordered by blighted houses, at the end of which stretched a park with lawns that were too vivid in color, like glowing red nailpolish at the end of soiled, dingy fingers.

They made slow progress, as though impeded in their movements by the warm, slightly moist air, and neither spoke. At the entrance of the park, there was a woman selling toys: little celluloid windmills, balls, dolls. He knew, without even having to look at her, that the child's eyes, inexpressive, already rather bulging eyes, like those of an insect, had turned towards the toys, only ever so slightly, since she didn't want to let it be seen, and he knew it, that she was looking at them. It seemed to him that an avid, frightened little animal was cowering inside her watching him slyly, and he felt, emanating from her, something like weak, flabby tentacles that fastened on to him timidly, palpating him. At this repellent contact he stiffened immediately and passed on, looking straight in front of him, without appearing to hear the guileless, placid toy woman who was trying to coax him to buy: "Right this way, sir, how about a toy for the little girl. . . . She'd be glad, wouldn't you, honey? she'd like to have a nice little windmill to play with. . . ."

But he would not be taken in. For nothing on earth would he have yielded. And as he dragged her away, pressing her little hand hard in his fingers, he experienced a sort of painful enjoyment, a bitter-tasting slightly cloying satisfaction, tearing from him and crushing the soft, flabby little tentacles that clung timidly to him.

When she entered the room, he didn't even turn his head in her direction. Bent over his desk, with an air of absorption, he pretended to be looking through his papers. He wore his old sullen expression, his face was inscrutable and heavy. To the conventional questions: "Well! how do you feel? Do you still feel grippy? How about those pains you were having? Have you been out of doors yet?" put to him in a tone that she tried to make sound natural, he replied with dull grunts. Who did she think she was fooling, anyway? already her voice sounded hollow. . . . He experienced

167

a sort of hateful joy as he felt her hesitate, a bit out of countenance, feeling her way, while he didn't budge . . . things had come to a pretty pass if he should have to help her out, make it easier for her. But he knew that even though he remain on his guard, and refuse to expose himself, it would be of no use, he would not be able to stop her, nor even to hold her off for long. She never lingered very long over preliminaries of pure form, over the practice thrusts, and, at present, she was watching him cautiously, on the lookout for the propitious moment.

And while she was hesitating and casting about, he felt rising within him and blending with his apprehension, with his desire to hold her off, a sort of impatient anticipation, the same anguish, the same impatience that was swelling in her, he felt it, and he was almost relieved when, unable to stand it any longer, she made up her mind: "Listen, papa, I've been wanting to talk to you. . . . You know I told you that I had been to see the doctor . . ." she was talking in her mealy-mouthed, falsely conciliatory tone. . . . He drew himself up suddenly, rearing back, his voice, too, had a hollow ring: "The doctor? What doctor? What do you mean doctor?"—"You know, I spoke to you about it; ever since I had that fall. . . . My leg doesn't seem to get well. . . . The doctor even wondered if it might not be tubercular. He said I needed treatment, orthopedic massage and x-rays. . . . I should have started a long time ago. . . . Everybody is surprised I haven't . . . Renée. . . ." Her head had already begun to wag, her face had flattened, her eyes were red, she was about to cry. . . . "The doctor seemed worried, he didn't seem at all optimistic when he examined the x-ray pictures. . . ." The old women around her shook their heads pityingly. . . . "Isn't that a downright shame" . . . they looked at him reproachfully . . . "and when you think that she's all he has in the world . . . one thing is certain, he can't take it with him. . . ."

But he wouldn't be taken in. Not he. They were not going to get a rise out of him. They'd wish they hadn't tried. . . . He, too, had his hard shell, his impregnable, protective armor . . . he turned towards her, his hands thrust in his pockets, well planted on his widespread feet—a big whale of a fellow, strong and determined not to let himself be imposed upon: "Ah! so it's Renée's doctor, is it? That homeopathist? That quack bone setter? How much does he want for his treatment? Ah! he's not the one who does it? And the masseur, I suppose he was the one who recommended him? And the x-rays? Oh, I know, I know them . . . I know their schemes for getting money out of suckers . . . all these good people who pass their time feeling their pulse: 'Have I got this? Have I got that?' You and your manias. . . . At your age, I had something better to do than to be running from one masseur to the other. As for our parents, at your age, we were the ones who helped them, yes, that's perfectly true . . . I saved on my bus fares —I always went up top, no matter what the weather—in order to send a little money to my mother. . . . No, indeed, we weren't like you are, we didn't spend our time patting ourselves to see if something was wrong . . . often I would make my lunch off of a bag of chestnuts. . . ." He remembered it as if it had been yesterday. . . . His old chum Jerome used to come along and stick his great blue hands into the bag. . . . No, indeed, we weren't like they are. We didn't count on our parents to help us. . . .

169

He was not alone, either, like her he had his protective cohort, his old guard, that he trotted out when things got too complicated, his old friends, who were always ready to stand by him . . . this time, as he fought, step by step, he felt them behind him—a firm rampart. . . . On Saturdays, when he went to meet good old Jerome at the restaurant —a first-class restaurant, because he too, the old codger, had come quite a way since those rides on top of the bus, he'd become "somebody," as they say—when he went to lunch with Jerome and a few old cronies of the old days, right away, just as soon as he passed through the revolving door into the inviting warmth and saw him, in his usual seat, waving his folded newspaper in greeting, the metamorphosis took place, relieving and slightly painful, just as shedding must be for insects. It was as though a vacuum cleaner had passed through him, picking up everything that was either floating about inside him, or palpitating at the slightest breath, all the diffused feelings of anguish, all the dubious strange impulses. Under their placid gaze, a manner they have that is so self-assured and always slightly indifferent, he felt that he filled up with a consistent substance that gave him density and weight, steadiness, he too became "somebody," protected and respectable, deeply rooted, stuck like a wedge in the well-constructed universe they lived in. Like everything else that surrounded them, the dining room with its broad comfortable seats and discreet lighting, as also the bill of fare and the well-trained waiters with their skillful, deferential manner, he assumed under their gaze simple, precise outlines, a reliable, familiar look (for those lunching at the nearby tables, one glance was enough to be able to catalogue him, he was

170

so definitely, from head to foot, in his entire bearing, in his gestures, a type, a character, but, let's see, out of what novel? they didn't know exactly, but at one glance, they identified him: a good standard garment copied from an old model).

Like the invisible threads that set marionettes in motion, the current from their glance directed each one of his movements, all those poised, lusty gestures that he felt himself making as he unfolded his napkin and studied the bill of fare with the reflective air of a connoisseur . . . the headwaiter, leaning respectfully towards him (for many years familiar with his generous tips and his simple good-nature . . . nothing upstage about him, no, sir!), studied the bill of fare with him: "The baked beans are very good today, sir . . . one of our specialties. . . ."—"So you want to kill me, eh? And what about arthritis, you don't know what that is, arthritis, do you, not yet, anyway?" The headwaiter smiled and looked him straight in the eyes, gray, piercing eyes, eyes that the headwaiter liked, ever since he had happened to see in them, one day as he watched the old man joking with one of the waiters, or patting the cheek of the cashier's little girl, or passing the time of day with the woman in the cloakroom, as she held his coat, a gleam of emotion, something fond and tender. "To start with, no bread. Toast, that's my new diet." The old cronies laughed: "Look at the old rake, the old beau! still thinking of his figure. . . ." Like water discovered by a divining rod, his good hearty laugh, embarrassed and flattered, burst out: Ho-ho-ho . . . I alone, if I had been at the very next table, would perhaps have noted—I'm so contrary-minded—in the last vibrations of that vanishing laugh, buried under

171

his drooping cheeks, a sort of vague reflection of that smile he has sometimes, secret and turned in on himself, a smile for him alone, that I am familiar with; but nobody around him could notice it, that rapid gleam that passes on to go and lose itself in him, bury itself at the bottom of a hole, like a mouse.

It was delightful, once the meal had been ordered with the greatest care—"the burgundy at room temperature, eh? above all, not like the last time, not like the last time!"— to turn to serious matters: the banks, Swiss investments, the latest tips on the Stock Exchange. . . . He was circumspect, our old fellow, well informed, nothing escaped him, always prudent, cunning, too prudent, in fact, too suspicious at times. . . . "Come along there, old boy, have a little enthusiasm, a little faith, a little rashness, what the devil!" They tapped him on the shoulder, laughing affectionately; but he was aware of the risks and the difficulties, he would never let himself be deluded. "As for phosphates, was I right to wait? not to buy? Tell me what they are worth now? The fact is that I can't, I'm not alone. I have responsibilities." But they approved, they understood. They had learned long ago, like him, to respect hard necessities, realities, ah! no, they would be the last ones to urge him to commit any sort of mad extravagance: "Of course, that's certain. . . . Children, they're what people work for and deprive themselves for, the ones they put money aside for. . . . However, your daughter, I thought . . . now mine, ever since she was married, I haven't had to worry. My son-in-law is a fine young fellow. A hard worker. 'Just give me five years, then you'll see . . .' he said that when I asked him: 'That's all very fine, but how about your future, my boy?'

172

. . . He kept his word. I don't have to help them any more now . . . oh, a few treats from time to time. . . . But you, for instance, you're too good, too indulgent, too weak, that's the word. They never show any gratitude, believe me. If you want a little appreciation for what you give them, keep them on short rations. As for me, I can tell you, when I was fourteen years old, my father said to me: 'Now, my boy, that's enough. You've played long enough. Your school days are over. Life is about to start.' It started all right, and it hasn't always been easy, but when all's said and done, we got along, didn't we, old chap, we got along some- how, just the same . . . oh, I can tell you, it has meant hard work, since the old days on the top deck of the bus, on the Montparnasse-Gare de l'Est line. . . . But still and all, we didn't get along too badly, did we?"

"No, sir! we weren't like you, we didn't count on our parents to shoulder all our burdens . . . Papa, I need this, or I need that. . . . When we were your age, and even well before then, it was our parents who leaned on us, that's absolutely true. . . ." But he was too generous, too weak. . . . One thing, however, he wouldn't let anybody come and remonstrate with him, that would be a little too much, or tell him what he should do. . . . No, not him. Well planted on his widespread feet, his hands thrust into his pockets, he grew stiff and heavy, opaque: the fellow with the clean-cut outlines that his friends had unfalteringly cut out of the solid substance that surrounded them. A man like them-selves, circumspect, settled. There was of course that mask he felt against his face, and that funny voice, slightly foggy, which he always has when he speaks to her, but that was nothing, he was holding his own: "What are you complain-

173

ing about, after all? What's this all about? You should have enough left over from what you get already. How many people are there, in our day, whose parents give them an income comparable to what I give you? How many, at your age? Do you know many?"

But they're in a militant mood, too, she and the fairies; they won't give in either, that's not the way they see it, "Well, really, what does he imagine . . . where does he think he is, anyway, that father of yours, in the moon?" She shook her head, overcome—"Isn't that a downright shame"—she too is strong, with clear-cut outlines: a poor, unfortunate woman struggling with hard necessity. . . . "How can you say that? You don't seem to realize how much more expensive everything has become. . . . Everybody knows that, for goodness sake, everybody is complaining about it, prices are absolutely exorbitant . . . the slightest thing. . . ."

Tstt—tstt—he was shaking his head with impatience, his hands, thrust deep in his pockets, were clinking his keys together . . . *tstt* . . . *tstt* . . . he knew all about that. . . . "No use coming with all kinds of excuses, I don't know who 'everybody' is, who has told you all that nonsense, but I do know something about prices. All that is just so much bunk. And even so, has my income increased? When the cost of living rises, I deny myself a few more things, that's all, the way I've always done . . . I don't count on the help of anybody; in fact, I never had anybody I could count on. . . ."

They were standing firmly, brow to brow, heavy and awkward, in their rigid carapaces, their heavy armor—two giant insects, two enormous dung beetles. . . . "I ask as little as possible from you, and you know it, it's no pleasure to ask anything at all from you . . . I ask for as little as possible, but still there are times . . . and yet it's perfectly natural. . . . Everybody thinks it's perfectly normal to turn to your father when there's an emergency like this . . . an accident . . . people are surprised, I can tell you, everybody understands that, you're the only one. . . ." —"Ah! indeed. So that's it. Don't wear yourself out. I know. I know that tune by heart. I know, I know all about it. I'm your father. You're my daughter . . . I'm all you have in the world. . . . Your rights." He felt his rage boiling up, a desire to take her and shake her, to tear off her mask too, that silly, flat face she makes, to crack that carapace she thinks she's so safe in, behind which she dares to defy him, to drag her out into the open, gasping and naked. . . . "But what's it all about, at bottom? What is the subject under discussion? What are all these lamentations leading up to? I like precise details. What's it all about? How much does that charlatan of yours want?" With the keen scent of a hunting dog that scratches and digs in the ground in order to make the little animal hiding deep down in its hole come out into the open, he sensed, by her hesitation, by the slight vibrations she emitted, that it was that. . . . He had touched the right spot. . . . He was breathing more heavily, his heart was beating faster, with excitement and impatience, and also with apprehension at the thought of what was going to appear suddenly, while he insisted, kept on: "How much? how much? Answer me. Well, go ahead and answer. . . ."

The trap door was lifted, they had lifted the trap door, the ground had opened up under their feet, they swayed on the brink of the abyss, they were about to fall in. . . . She felt herself pulling back with a sort of flabby wrench: "Six

175

thousand francs. . . . He told me it would cost around six thousand francs." He stuck his head forward a bit, half-closing his eyes, he was articulating emphatically, as though dumbfounded, stressing each syllable: "Six thousand francs? Six thou-sand francs. . . ?" They were slipping, attached to each other, they were falling. . . . She heard him laugh: "Six thousand francs! For massage! That's all!"

Just as Alice in Wonderland, after she had drunk the contents of the magic vial, felt that she was changing form, shrinking, then growing taller, it seemed to them that their outlines were breaking up, stretching in every direction, their carapaces and armors seemed to be cracking on every side, they were naked, without protection, they were slipping, clasped to each other, they were going down as into the bottom of a well . . . the fairies, the old cronies, already far behind, had remained up there, on the surface, in the daylight . . . down where they were going now, things seemed to wobble and sway as in an undersea landscape, at once distinct and unreal, like objects in a nightmare, or else they became swollen, took on strange proportions . . . six thousand francs . . . a great flabby mass was weighing on her, crushing her . . . she tried clumsily to disengage herself a bit, she heard her own voice, a funny, too neutral-sounding voice. . . . "I believe it's an inclusive price. The gymnastic lessons, the ultraviolet rays, all that is included. In fact, it's a special price for me. Last year, after her ski accident in Mégève, Renée . . ." at this point these words sounded very funny indeed, words from out yonder, used by people who live somewhere very far away, as though on another planet, in a universe with other dimensions, the words of people who walk in the sunlight, loiter in front of shopwindows, buy a newspaper, absent-mindedly throw a coin on the pile of newspapers and pass on, whistling. . . . She didn't understand through what stupid oversight, through what aberration she could have for one moment allowed herself to believe that she was like them, one of them. . . . If they had come near her now, the fairies or Renée, she would have turned her head, abashed. . . . And he, if they had decided his old cronies— but they were far away—if they could have come to pull him by the tail of his jacket to try and bring him back to them: "Why it's nothing serious, come on, there's really no reason why you should get into such a state, it's nothing really, it's not worth-while mentioning, it's nothing serious, old boy . . ." he would have pushed them aside impatiently, they should let him alone, he had no use in this instance for their ponderous common sense, he would have rejected with rage, trampled underfoot the cardboard armor with its commonplace outlines with which they tried to disguise him; this was not the time, he needed all his liberty of movement, this time the cup was full, her audacity had gone too far, he could hardly believe it . . . six thousand francs . . . for massage . . . was that all? Indeed? . . . he began to laugh . . . it would be a crime, if he didn't straighten out matters right away, a crime was about to be committed, the most serious of all, the only unpardonable crime here in this world, in the world into which they had both de-scended, this world of theirs in which both of them were now imprisoned. . . .

It had been in order for her to learn to avoid all temptation ever to commit that crime that he had accustomed her, at a very tender age, to advance only by short, regular steps,

eyes on the ground, huddled up close to him, frightened.
. . . It was for that reason, in order for her to be well
trained, that he had passed by—for that too, I feel sure,
though at the time I hadn't realized it, one can't be everywhere at once, each word they speak, the most apparently
insignificant of their movements, is like a crossroads
traversed by innumerable roads leading in every direction,
and I have arrived at this point without knowing exactly
how, after a long roundabout way—it was for that reason,
in order to teach her to walk straight, as he said, that he had
passed on without turning his head in the direction of the
toys, the celluloid dolls and the little windmills; for that, in
order to nip in the bud the dangerous impulse he had already felt in her; for that, he had dragged her away, looking
straight in front of him, holding her tight, crushing her
little hand in his fingers.

It was for that, that they had walked, she trotting along
beside him, on the endless avenues, the broad, dusty
avenues, bordered with gray sycamores, in certain southern
towns, stopping to catch their breath, setting down the
heavy suitcases, while he mopped his forehead, without appearing to notice the carriages for hire that passed slowly
by. . . . They had been making difficult progress under the
jeering gaze of the coachman. . . . "Wouldn't the gent like
to get in and ride?" But they did not get in; they had pretended not to notice some people who were standing on the
curb motioning to the coachman, and they had felt, as they
continued their way, that they had been given a whack on
the back when they had heard behind them the little dry
mocking sound of the carriage door being closed.

Thus he had succeeded in developing in her little by

178

little—but she was perhaps born with it, she had perhaps already inherited it from him—a sort of special sense, similar to his own, which permitted her to perceive immediately, hidden everywhere, this sort of threat, known only to them, the danger that dwells in each object, however harmless in appearance, like a wasp in the heart of a fruit.

Just as a dog, whose master has taught him to follow at heel by pulling pitilessly on the leash each time that he loiters or, attracted by various odors, tries to get away, when he is no longer on leash, feels the old pinch of the collar around his neck, calling him sharply to order as soon as he strays a bit from the path, she felt now, even when away from him, as soon as she let herself go a bit, as soon as she stretched out her hand timidly, let her fingers linger over the thick, too smooth paper of a magazine lying on the counter in a bookshop, or even lifted one foot imprudently towards the step of a bus, while the conductor, his arm in the air, ready to ring the bell, told her, in a tone in which she seemed to hear a warning, a challenge, aimed just at her: "Only first-class seats left . . ." she felt, as before, pulling her back, the sharp tightening of the leash and the collar cutting her flesh.

It had been through exercise, through constant training, by pulling constantly on the leash, without ever relaxing his vigilance, that he had succeeded in training her to be like that. Only through exercise, as a result of constant practice. The crime itself, that he had taught her to dread above all others, he had never openly designated. Never had he dared call it by name. They felt, both of them, that it would be already committing it simply to pronounce this name in thought. . . . If a cynically bold, or simply unaware person had ever taken the liberty of mentioning it before them, they would have lowered their eyes, frightened, ashamed, they would have stopped up their ears. I myself, down here where I am with them now, hardly dare pronounce it under my breath. . . . Offhandedness . . . I think that's how it is called . . . offhandedness . . . the crime they never have dared call by name. . . . It cast its immense shadow over the world in which they lived; it covered their world entirely like a giant netting with invisible, finely woven meshes—as soon as she tried timidly to make the slightest movement, as soon as she began to quiver a little, or to try to disengage herself, she felt its tightened meshes covering her on all sides—or rather, it would be more exact to compare the crime that he was constantly dangling before her to the black liquid that an octopus sprays about itself to blind its prey. . . . "Corsica? Indeed? Italy? And why not China? Why not a trip around the world, eh? Why not? Ah! mountain climbing? The latest fad? The Meije, Mount Blanc? And your outfit? That can come later, eh? We'll think about that afterwards, we'll speak of that later, you can't be bothered with such trifles, isn't it so? But I happen to know what such an outfit costs, with the hotel and all the rest. . . . But you, of course, you hadn't thought about that, it doesn't bother you. . . . The goose that laid the golden egg, that's what I am for you, it just falls from heaven like manna, you can afford anything. . . . Six thousand francs . . . that's all . . . for beauty treatments. . . . Ha! anybody can see that you have never done anything with your two hands. . . . Six thousand francs. . . ." He was shouting. ". . . do you know how hard you would have to work to earn that amount? That's the salary of a civil servant, or a judge; as for myself, I remember how I had to slave, how I had to economize; but little you care, do you? You would bring me to a pauper's grave, if you had your way, absolutely destitute, a pauper's grave. . . ."

"A pauper's grave, indeed. . . !" She laughed with his same laughter, an icy, false laughter. " . . . So I'll bring you to a pauper's grave! You say that to me. . . . When I myself have just about one foot in the grave. Seriously. No, I'm not just talking, the doctor was anxious . . . I've already waited too long . . . I'm sure he suspected bone tuberculosis, and I look so badly that people are afraid of me, everybody has noticed it, I'm growing thinner every day. . . . But little you care, and no mistake, after all, I can go to a public hospital, can't I, I can be treated at a free clinic, that's plenty good enough for me . . . that's where I'll end . . . I knew all along that that was where I would end one day, if I should ever fall ill, people like me go to a public hospital, people who have nothing that belongs to them, nobody they can count on. To a public hospital, that's where I'll go, that's where I can go and die like a dog. . . ."

His own ludicrous image. A caricature of himself—that flat, protruding face, those already red eyes, about to water, that mouth twisted into an expression of bitter hatred and shame, his expression—his own image ridiculously overdone, and distended, as in a deforming mirror. . . . No, there was no danger. Not with her. Never. What had he been thinking about? And I myself, what flights of the imagination had I indulged in? What had I been talking about? What offhandedness? No, really, he had nothing to fear about that. Never, even in her innermost thoughts, had she dared break away from him all at once and escape to the outside world, tearing the meshes of the netting. Clinging to him timidly, huddled up to his side, her docile little hand held tight in his big hand, she had never for a single moment dreamed of drawing away from him, but on the contrary, had always remained turned towards him, riveted to him, watching his every movement, every change of expression, following with her eyes, as though fascinated, wherever he looked. And then she saw, suddenly appearing before them, like the great rocks that the passengers of a ship in distress see emerging from time to time from out of the fog, hideous, threatening shapes. If she had merely glanced in a detached, innocent manner at these phantoms, if she had turned her head away casually, perhaps they would have vanished . . . she would have driven them off the way the morning sun drives off obsessions of the night. But she had stared at them, she couldn't take her eyes, that were stretched so wide they were about to crack, off of them, she recognized them immediately: Sickness, Poverty, Ruin, Failure. . . . Enormous, crushing masses . . . there they stood all about them . . . they barred all exits, like the giant statues, wearing frightening masks and uttering lugubrious groans, that guarded the entrance to the strange country of Erewhon and made terrified travelers retrace their paths.

A parasite. A leech. Glued to him, without ever having torn herself away from him for a single instant, she had never ceased to breathe in avidly everything that emanated from him. She had never allowed anything to go unused, not a scrap did she scorn. It was she, he knew, who had always brought out in him all the things that he would have liked to hold back, his fear, that shameful fear that he would have liked to hide, but she had felt it pulsing faintly within him and had made it spurt forth—an acrid, thick blood that she had fed upon.

Now she was right up against him, soaked heavy with fear. His own foul droppings. Loathsome. . . . He clenched his fists and began to shout, but the words that came bursting up seemed to have as little connection with the confused feelings that were boiling deep down inside him, as the will-o'-the-wisps that dance on the opaque surface of stagnant water have with the invisible, complicated process of decomposition of the plants that lie underneath the ooze on the bottom of a pond: "No, none of that. . . . Nobody is to make a fool of me, do you hear me, I don't like to be taken for any stupider than I am. . . . Go tell that to your girl friends. . . . Don't try to tell that to me, I know you too well. . . . There's one thing I know that they certainly don't know, those girl friends of yours, you didn't tell them everything. . . . There's one thing they don't know, but that I do know, I know you. . . . You don't need that money. No, it's not true, you have no need at all for it. . . . By dragging it out of me, one sou at a time, you have got together quite a little pile, haven't you? Did you tell them that? Only your pile means more to you than your own hide. For nothing on earth would you touch that. With my money you can afford such things as massage and beauty treatments—exactly, I know what I'm talking about —but your own savings, eh, well that's something sacred, that can't be touched. . . ." She drew herself up, her rigid face thrust forward, she was speaking in that choked voice of hers, at once caustic and affected, slightly rolling her r's: "Please excuse me if I laugh. . . . So it's you . . . now, it's you, is it, who are reproaching me with having saved a little money. . . . It would have been better for me if I had . . . I wouldn't be so hard up now, just when I find myself in an emergency. . . . But you may rest assured, I have nothing. Not a sou. I'd like to know how I could have done it, when I can never make out till the end of each month. I deny myself everything. I had to cancel my coal order this winter, when I saw the price. I have nothing to wear, I never go out. I barely have enough to eat. . . ."

Of course, there was no need to tell that to him, he knew her, always depriving herself, cutting down on everything, continually snooping and poking about, nosing around everywhere, looking for ways to save a few sous. . . . Never a moment of entertainment, she wouldn't indulge herself. . . . Never a gesture of loathing, nothing discouraged her, embarrassment was something she had forgotten, she was ready to face anything. . . . He had sometimes been ashamed of her before other people, even when she was still young; the looks the people around them gave one another, the looks of the servants in hotels, when he had had the misfortune to ask her to do the tipping, their meager, protracted smile, the way he had felt them staring after him; but she was so thick-skinned, she didn't care a rap, nothing mattered to her, as soon as it was a question of saving a few sous. . . . And this sort of promiscuity, this sort of loathsome complicity that she caused to exist between them, that she forced upon him—it was on purpose, he knew, in order to debase him slyly, to lower him—as when she would hand him a bill, commenting on it scathingly in her slangy, derisive way: "This guy makes no bones about it. If you want what he's got, you've gotta pay for it. And the workmen's time . . . that alone. . . ." What loathing she had aroused in him when he had watched her—that was long ago, she was still a child at the time—go and hide the bag of candy she had received for Christmas, before her little friends arrived. . . . It was doubtless this, the fact of seeing her like that all the time, her nose to the ground, cringing and trembling, that awakened and made rise up in protest within him something that had been lying dormant, a drowsy animal, a wild, cruel animal, ready to leap at her and bite. . . . If she had ever raised her head in disdain and cast an absent-minded gaze elsewhere, perhaps the beast in him—like a dog that stops barking and retires, calmed down, when the passer-by he was attacking goes on his way, unperturbed—perhaps the beast in him would have fallen asleep again; but he saw her there at his feet, cringing, crawling in the mud and the mire; there she was before him, flaccid, acquiescent, always within reach; the temptation was too great, an irresistible desire was growing in him to seize hold of her, to bend her double, to batter her down, further still, harder. . . . "But my poor girl, I know you, a gold mine, El Dorado itself, do you hear me, all the gold of Croesus, nothing would change you, I could give you anything on earth, you would still deprive yourself of everything, you would let yourself die of hunger, just to be able to put more and more money aside . . . you like to do it, I know you, you're like that, you can't do without it. . . ."

"Well, I must say, that's going too far . . . !" All at once her eyes filled with tears. ". . . that's really too hard. . . ."

She was on the verge of a scene, she had that air of helpless anger of a child who is about to "go into a tantrum"—"You dare say that to me, it's you who say that to me! That's going too far! You know perfectly well"—all at once she had softened, her eyes were streaming—"you know perfectly well I wouldn't be like that if I had been brought up differently, you are the one who gave me the habit. . . ." Her flat face and dejected air gave her the look of a weeping widow. . . . She did it on purpose, it was to make him feel ashamed, he knew that, in order to humiliate him, to make people feel sorry for her at his expense, that she got herself up the way she did, with her black lisle-thread stockings and her darned gloves, so that she could throw that into his face: you made me what I am, you wanted it, I am your product, your handiwork. . . .

He could have taken her in his two hands and crushed her. . . . "Ah! so it's me now, so I'm the cause of all your woes, I'm your scapegoat. . . . I can tell you I'm beginning to have about enough, I've shouldered the blame for too long, I've had enough. . . ." He was hesitating, he was looking around him for something to crush her with, but there was nothing within reach, he found nothing at hand, except such coarse, heavy-to-handle contrivances as are used by the people up there—he sensed confusedly that this was not what was needed here, between them, they didn't need crude instruments borrowed from those other people out there, but it couldn't be helped, he saw nothing else, he had no choice. . . . "You ought to look around a bit, catch yourself another victim. . . . Find yourself a husband, what the hell. . . . A husband. . . . It's high time. . . ." He felt that he was crushing a flabby substance that was yielding

186

and into which he was sinking. . . . "When you need that badly to be carried along on somebody's outstretched arms, or live like a parasite, always clinging to somebody else, you look for a husband. A husband. . . . Then it would be his turn. . . . Only . . ." he was sinking further and further down, he was being dragged down, meeting with no resistance . . . "only, there's nobody around, eh? nobody wants the job, I take it! Ah, ha! there haven't been any bidders yet . . ." he was experiencing the painful, sickening voluptuousness of a maniac, the kind that takes one's breath away, that one feels when one presses one's own abscess between two fingers to make the pus spurt out, or when one tears off bit by bit the scab of a wound . . . "they don't want the job, they're no fools . . ." he was choking, his words came with difficulty . . . "for them there's nothing doing . . ." he was going down, he was sinking as though from dizziness, drawn further and further down, to the depths of a strange voluptuousness, a funny sort of voluptuousness that resembled suffering: "Ah! it's because she's too homely, if you must know . . . she's too homely . . . and it's probably I too, I who forced you . . . I who am responsible for your looks. . . ."

She struggled feebly, gave a few kicks without really trying to disengage herself, hitting out the while in a mild way that increased his excitement; she started talking in her weepy, slightly childish, exasperating voice. . . . "Yes, it's you, of course it's you, you did everything you could to keep me by myself, so that I should see nobody, you always kept me from seeing people, or going out . . . what scenes you used to make if I ever made so bold as to invite anyone for dinner . . . I looked like a servant girl, I was dressed

like a servant girl, I didn't dare let anybody see me. . . ."
He took a little time off to tighten his hold, get a more convenient grip on her, he had all the time he needed, there
she was in his hands, inert, one might have said that she was
waiting. . . . He sneered . . . "Naturally . . . I was sure of
it . . . that's nothing new . . . I'm the unfeeling brute . . .
I'm the ogre who kept the suitors from crowding around
to sue for happiness. . . ." One moment more . . . before
letting himself fall further down, to the bottom this time,
to the very bottom. . . . "No, my poor girl, just between
ourselves, eh? No, but can't you see for yourself, tell me,
have you ever looked at yourself . . ." the abscess had burst,
the scab was entirely off, the wound was bleeding, suffering
and voluptuousness had attained their peak, he was at the
end of his tether, at the very end, they had reached bottom,
alone together, they were by themselves, now they were
quite by themselves, naked, stripped, far from outside
eyes . . . he felt steeped in the atmosphere of mellowness,
the relaxed tepidity produced by intimacy—alone in their
nice, big hide-out, where you can do anything you want,
where there is no longer any need to conceal anything—he
was holding her by the lapel of her coat, talking right close
up to her face. . . . "Well, if you want to know, I never
did speak to you about it, but since you force me to do so
now, well, I'm going to tell you . . . if you want to know the
truth, I did everything, I tell you, everything and more
still. . . . You remember that Adonis, that young fellow . . .
you know perfectly well who I'm talking about . . . well,
I all but crawled to get him to marry you, I made up to
him, I even went so far as to sink money in that little business of his . . . but as for him, there was nothing doing . . .

he left, you remember. . . ." He looked at her a bit from one side, his voice was slightly hoarse. . . . "He left, he cut and ran . . . in other words, nothing came of it. . . ."

Our Hypersensitive. . . . Who would have recognized her now? She who trembled at the slightest breath, who quivered and withdrew into herself at the slightest contact, took these blows without batting an eyelash. A barely visible something about her that resembled quaking, a slight unsteadiness—almost nothing. . . . She blushed a little, just as a matter of form, she too was speaking right up close to him, her voice too was low, hoarse: "Well, believe it or not, I've got something to tell you, too. . . . I've been hesitating thus far, but now my mind is made up. . . . You won't have much longer to carry me on your outstretched arms, as you say . . . you'll soon be rid of me. . . . There's no accounting for tastes. . . . Imagine, if you can, that there's a nice man who would like to make his life with me. We've waited a long while, but our minds are about made up . . . I can speak to you about it now . . . we are going to become engaged. . . ." En-gaged. . . . She pronounced the word awkwardly, with a childish, silly air about her. . . . Always the same words from up there, the same contrivances, heavy and hard to handle, intended for the use of the people up there, the only ones they have at hand. Now I saw it. I knew it. I saw it all at once clearly, the secret of her attitude—so surprising at first glance to anyone who knew her —underneath his telling blows, the secret of her insensibility to suffering that reminded one of the almost miraculous impassibility of the early Christian martyrs—Saint Blandina submitting to torture with complete serenity: all of their gestures, all of their movements, those she was trying to make at that moment, and which were copies of the ones people make up there, on the surface, in daylight, seemed now—in that dark, entirely closed world in which they were both confined, in that world of their own in which they went eternally round and round, lighter in weight, childish and harmless, as different from those made by the people on the outside, as are the leaps and bounds, the flights and pursuits of a ballet from those of everyday life.

The games they played . . . their gnawings and nibblings . . . the sweet taste of nourishing milk. The soft warmth of the breast. The familiar, bland and slightly sugary odor of their intimacy. . . . She smelled it, I am sure, she inhaled it voluptuously, shut up snugly in there with him, when he held her so tight, and whispered so close to her things that only they knew, when he bowled her over, far from the sight of others, with what he called his "truths." It had been that same taste, that same secret odor that she had relished already, and had delighted in, in the past—I had sensed it confusedly—when they used to walk (here I am back again, each one of their gestures, each word they speak is like a knot in which a thousand tangled threads are inextricably mingled together), when they used to pass on, without turning their heads to look at cabs and windmills, timidly close together, huddled up to each other under the curious, insolent gaze of strangers, her damp, little hand curled tightly in his big hot hand. . . . Their hide-out. Their nice, big hide-out. . . . It was only to get him a little more excited that she struggled like that, that she tried to answer back, that she pretended she wanted to break away from him. It was just to tease him.

Perhaps, too, to get at him, somewhere in the depths of his being, in a sensitive spot that she knew well, a secret spot known only to them.

Now he tightened his grip. Held her closer and tighter, as always, each time she looked as if she wanted to break away from him, or try to escape from him—he never loosened his hold, he was there, still, on the watch . . . as soon as she budged, at the slightest movement, he drew her savagely towards him—he held her close up against him, they were clinging one to the other, in their insipid, warm odor, entirely enveloped by heavy fumes, he pointed out to her, emerging and rising up all about them, guarding all exits, threatening forms, wearing hideous masks, uttering frightening groans, he had the delightful sensation, while she snuggled up against him—as formerly, when she used to follow, riveted to him, the direction of his eyes— of feeling the gentle palpitations of her heart beating in unison with his own. . . .

But then . . . it seemed to me all at once, as I watched him hurl himself at her and try to tear up what she was dangling before his eyes to excite him, that there was nothing in him but blind impulse, a sort of opaque fury that filled him entirely, a fury like that of a bull when it charges, head down, against the cape held out by the matador: "Ha! indeed! So he's back on the scene again? That affair's still going on? It's that fellow again? He's the famous suitor, is he? He's come to your rescue again? So he's back, is he, that guy from the Finance Ministry? He's your sheet anchor now? your protector? Only, I'd like to know with what he plans to found this happy home, this little Paradise of his? Not, I imagine, with only his salary? Because you'll have to live, won't you, and perhaps, even, several of you, he must know that better than I do . . . I don't believe he's going to be satisfied, nor you either, eh? from what I know of you, with love in a cottage. . . . And that's why, in an emergency, you'll come whining . . . you'll come and whine that you're broke at the end of every month . . . this time you'll really find out what privation means, and no joking, for good, the way I did, I know all about it. . . . But he's no fool, that guy, he must know what he's about, he's probably counting on a nice neat little sum that will permit him to leave that skimpy life of his behind, 'begin a new life,' as you say, otherwise, believe me. . . ."

She lifted her head high, in a way that I had never seen her do, and turned aside with a disdainful air: "Well, that's where you are mistaken. Believe it or not, he doesn't want anything. He doesn't want to ask you for anything. . . . He is not counting on anybody but himself. . . ."

I don't know what I could have been thinking when I said that she would only have to raise her head well above the miasmas into which he tried to push her, to impress him and command his respect. . . . But he didn't seem to take her seriously, he was not going to be taken in by her air of detachment, by this unusual display of dignity; it was too late, he knew her, let her put on airs if she wanted to, he would not let himself be deluded. . . .

Or perhaps, on the other hand, he suddenly had the impression that it was true. That she had suddenly taken a leap. A real one—like the ones they take up there, on the surface, in daylight. A leap in order to get out of his reach. . . . Perhaps he had noticed, perhaps he had suddenly seen beside her not the ridiculous puppet that I myself thought

I saw, the scarecrow that I saw, but something alive, a creature of flesh and blood, a thick, heavy, threatening presence, that sustained her, drew her to it, towards which she was straining, on which she was leaning in order to mock him—an enemy facing him, defying him. . . . He charged: "Ah! he doesn't want anything? He doesn't want anything, isn't that just fine!"—he was imitating her simper—"He's not counting on anybody but himself—a real hero, a noble soul, a perfect gentleman. . . . But I happen to know what all these fine intentions are going to cost me . . . I know what all these high and mighty airs will come to, in the long run. . . ." He sneered: "I know all about it. . . ." She raised her head even higher: "No, make no mistake, he knows what I have been through . . . I have talked to him frankly, he wants to take me away from it all." It seemed to me that he flinched ever so slightly. One might say that something in him wavered a bit. . . . He spoke with difficulty, in a jerky, staccato voice: "Ah! I see . . . you have confided in him. . . . You have unburdened yourself . . . at my expense. . . . What a fool you are. . . . Don't you see what his game is . . . you don't understand anything at all. . . . Ah! he knows what he's about. . . . Just think, it's a god-send. . . . Oh! he's in no hurry . . . he can wait. . . . Naturally. . . . You have hopes for the future . . . I'm a good investment. . . . And he hopes not to have to wait too long. . . . So you told him everything . . . you were obliged to let him know . . ." he looked around him with a distracted expression in his eyes . . . "you told him, eh, what you are hatching up. . . ." She nodded her head without saying anything, she seemed out of countenance, even a bit frightened. . . . "Oh, keep quiet, you can't fool me, I know, I see

193

everything, I know what you're after when you listen at keyholes, or when you go through my papers. . . . You have been through my checkbooks . . ." he took hold of her by the shoulders . . . "You are spying on me . . . you think I don't know it . . . you read my letters . . . oh, yes you do, I know it, there's no use sneering . . . you can't fool me, not me, I see everything, I know, you question people, you supervise my private life . . ." he laughed with a false laugh, enough to "give you the creeps," like the laugh of a lunatic. . . . "Ah! ah! I know you, you're scared to death, aren't you . . ." He shook her. ". . . you're scared to death at the thought that I too might start a new life. After all, I've a right to, don't you think? you've spoiled this one, all right . . . but you are afraid things will change, you are afraid of competition, you sweat fear as soon as you scent any danger from that direction, all you want is for me to pop off before. . . . You think I don't understand, you think I didn't know what was going through your head, eh? the last time, when I was sick. . . . It's not enough for you to rob me little by little, no, that's not enough, you're waiting for me to die, so you can feed on me, fatten on me. . . ." He shook her as hard as he could, shouting: "But I've had enough, enough, do you hear me, I also want to live my life, the way it suits me, I want people to leave me alone . . . I want you to leave me god-damned well alone once and for all, you and your stooge, that dirty louse of yours. . . ." He was stifling . . . "your pimp. . . ." He pushed her against the door. . . . He lowered his voice somewhat and began to talk right up close to her, in a hissing voice: "You're going to get the hell out of here, you're going to get out of here right away, do you hear me, and this time it'll be for

good, I don't want to see you again, get out, get out. . . !"
He opened the door with one hand while, with the other,
he held her, pushing her. She put up a resistance, set her
back against the wall, clutched hold of the door frame with
both hands, and all at once shouted, she too, for the first
time, in that caustic, mocking, provoking voice of hers:
"Ah! so that's it. . . . You've got what you were after . . . I
should have guessed it . . . that's what you were after from
the very beginning. . . . That's why you kept egging me
on. . . . So as not to have to part with it. . . ." She shouted
in a high, shrill voice: "This way, you can keep your money.
. . ." He gave her a blow in the chest that made her
let go of the door frame. . . . "You bitch. . . ! You dirty
bitch. . . !" He pushed her so hard that she bumped against
the front door just opposite the door of the study.

The concierge who was listening, while pretending to
polish the doorbell, or wipe the stair rail, must have been
startled, must have drawn back. The study door was heard
to slam, then there was the sound of the key in the lock. He
had locked the door.

An immense silence fell over the vestibule. An immense
silence and an immense chill. The only sound to be heard
was the furtive rubbing of the dustcloth which the concierge, in order to keep herself in countenance, was passing
over the wall, while she prudently stepped down one or
two steps. And, from the kitchen, the shrill, arrogant little
noise of plates being slipped one on top of the other by
the maid, her head bent slightly forward towards the half-
open door. Noises, in this silence, as alarming and threatening as the distant sound of a tam-tam.

But she had already pulled herself together; with a

bound, she seized the knob of the study door and turned it softly. Leaning against the keyhole, she whispered: "Let me in, papa, look, that's not reasonable . . . open the door. . . . What's the matter with you, anyway? Go ahead, open the door, I can't leave like this. . . . Hurry and open the door, this is ridiculous, people are listening. . . ." She turned the knob. . . . Her voice assumed a more and more childish, cry-baby tone. . . . "Let me in, listen. . . . It's embarrassing . . . people are listening. . . . You can't let me go like this . . . I'm ill. . . ." She was crying. . . . "It's serious. . . . More serious than you think. . . . Everybody knows that . . . I have already promised the doctor . . . papa . . . papa, listen to me. . . . Let me in . . . I'll explain it to you. I've had to take a loan . . . I've already paid a deposit. . . ." She rattled the knob. . . . "I absolutely must have it . . . I'll stay here as long as I have to . . . I can't leave like this. . . ."

Will he. . . . Won't he. . . . Will he. . . ? The key turned in the lock and the door opened, just wide enough for an arm to appear. A sort of choked shout was heard. . . . "What the hell. . . !" or "Go to hell. . . !" it was hard to distinguish exactly. . . . He stuck his arm through the crack in the door—he must have been holding the door to with the other hand—and threw a small wad of crumpled bank notes onto the carpet. . . . She gave a jump. Picked them up. Her face, as she straightened up, holding the bills, expressed satisfaction and relief. She unfolded them, started counting. There were four of them. . . . Four thousand-franc notes. . . . She nodded, smiling with a funny, knowing smile, half touched, half disdainful. She stuck the money into her bag, opened the front door gently. . . . The con-

196

cierge, her back turned, busily cleaning the bars of the staircase, stepped a bit to one side, to let her pass.

Not the slightest discomfiture did she show this time, nor did she tremble at all when she saw me appear before her suddenly on the sidewalk, as soon as she set foot out of the house. On the contrary, I was the one who was embarrassed, her cold expression made me lower my eyes and kept me at a distance. I tried timidly to buttonhole her, asked her in which direction she was going: I wanted to follow her, at all costs, wherever she was going. She felt this probably, but it didn't seem to bother her, or hardly, perhaps, just a vague tickle, a fly that lights on an elephant. She looked at her wrist watch: "Oh! my goodness, it's late. I wanted to go to the Manet exhibition. Tomorrow's the last day. But I'm very late."—"The Manet exhibition? It closes tomorrow, already? I should like to see it too. . . . I should hate to miss it. . . ." I was hesitating. Now it was my voice— reduced to a fine thread—that had assumed an affected, childish intonation: "May I go with you? You don't mind?" She turned her eyes in my direction, examining me quietly: "Certainly not. . . . Why should I? Only, we must hurry. It's late."

We walked fast, taking the curbings together with long strides, cutting corners. I trotted along beside her, as before, staring at her profile. Her austere outstretched head seemed to cleave the air like a ship's prow. No, not a prow; something hideous. Her head, thrust forward on the end of her rigid neck, made you think of the head of a gargoyle. No, not that, either. At present these words had an insipid, flat taste, that was slightly sickening. . . . Warmed over . . . I realized that, in spite of myself, out of sheer habit, as a result of overfatigue, mechanically, I was still cudgeling my brains. I was like a bicycle rider who, once the race is over and he is comfortably seated, continues, without being able to stop, to move his legs as though he were still pedaling away along the highroad. No, it's not that at all, either. An impartial, fresh observer might have seen in the dry line of her profile a certain purity, perhaps even nobility, almost a certain beauty. Or rather, it must be admitted that, for a detached observer, there was in her entire bearing, in her features, something unobtrusive and retiring, on the whole, something rather harmless, insignificant. With that schoolbag of hers hanging over her arm, she might have been mistaken for an overripe student, or a schoolteacher. And in fact, it was this picture of her that the mirrors in front of the shops and bars we passed gave back to us.

I did not look at them, except for an occasional rapid glance. As I trotted along beside her, I avoided looking at the fellow "beyond his prime," with the bedraggled air and short legs, balding and slightly pot-bellied. But occasionally, I was unable to avoid him. He sprang forth from a mirror just opposite me, as we crossed a street. Never had my weary lids, my dull eyes, my sagging cheeks, appeared to me so pitilessly as at that moment, beside her reflection, in that garish light.

She, too, saw it in the mirror, that reflection with the flabby, somewhat sloppy lines—the unwholesome fruit of obscure occupations and dubious ruminations, what, in fact, did he do all day? what did he do with his time? she

198

must have wondered vaguely. This picture tallied so exactly with the one she had retained of me that she experienced no surprise: she didn't even need to turn to look at me, as I did at her, in order to be sure of the resemblance. She had seen me like that for a long time. She knew me. She must have seen very clearly, too, the touching efforts that I still made, as formerly, to try to come a little nearer to her, she must have been amused by the man-about-town, lively tone that I assumed in spite of myself: "This year's exhibitions . . . they were really very interesting. . . . The El Grecos . . . did you see them? I'd like to know what you thought . . . I don't know whether you are like me, but I must admit that I was disappointed. . . . All those rather insipid pinks and lavenders . . . the whole thing seemed monotonous to me, almost a bit too vapid. . . ." She gave me a glance of slight astonishment: "Why, that's funny . . . I thought they were very good. . . . Some, in fact, were marvelous. . . ."

We had arrived. I saw her take a card out of her bag and walk ahead to the ticket window; she was determined not to let me pay for her ticket. Her head stretched towards the window, I saw her blushing deeply in evident rage: "What do you mean, it's no longer good? That's really too much! It's still perfectly good . . . I go everywhere with it. . . . For goodness sake . . . I'd just like to see such a thing. . . ." There was something too angry, too aggressive and hateful about her tone that was also aimed at me, that was aimed especially at me. I heard the ticket seller say calmly: "You can go ask the director, if you want to, but I can't let you in with that." She hesitated. She was embarrassed by my presence. Or rather no, on the contrary, it was my presence that made her feel she "would not be treated like that," that she was not going to "let herself be bluffed;" she would have liked to show me that she "didn't give a damn" what I might think, that she was not going to listen to any talk of refinement or squeamishness; we had our feet on the ground and she, for one, was through with childish nonsense, she wanted to give me a lesson. . . . But instead, she gave in, threw her money on the counter and with that slightly disreputable drawl of hers said: "All right, all right, let it go . . ." and moved on quickly without waiting for me. I hurried to get my ticket and joined her as she was about to enter the first room.

We walked slowly through the various rooms. From time to time she would stop before one of the canvases and stand stiffly, as though at attention. Respectfully, I too would come to a halt beside her, arms dangling and fingers clutching the brim of my hat, silent and earnest looking, as though in church. While she stared at the picture, I felt that there was a corner of her eye that remained turned on me, I did not leave the field of her vision. It seemed to me that she was challenging me again, from below. There was something between her and these pictures that resembled an alliance, a complicity aimed at me: I felt confusedly that they offered her, for use against me, something that she caught on the tip of her gaze, and which she tried to pass on to me, in order to set me straight again. As I stood there stiffly at her side, before them, I felt like a schoolboy whose teacher has made him hold a ruler across his back and under his arms, in order to force him to stand up straight.

All at once, she turned towards me and, with puckered

lips, let out an arrogant little whistle, accompanied by a nod and a look that meant: "That's it, eh? What do you think of it?" Her keen-edged whistle went right through me—one of those precise, sure aims that she knows how to take—and I now felt riveted to her side, rather like an insect that has been pinned down to the bottom of its glass-covered box.

This time, I gave a sort of weak start and began to struggle a bit. I tried to look her straight in the eye. . . . "Yes, . . . of course. I must admit, however, that it leaves me rather cold. . . . Undoubtedly, it is extremely good, but it's not what I like best. . . ." I felt myself blushing. . . . "It lacks disquiet . . . a certain . . . I mean to say . . . tremor . . . one feels in it too much assurance . . . too much satisfied certainty . . . or . . . perhaps . . . complacency. . . . I believe that rather than the most perfectly finished works I prefer those in which complete mastery has not been attained . . . in which one still feels, just beneath the surface, a sort of anxious groping . . . a certain doubt . . . a mental anguish . . ." I was beginning to splutter more and more . . . "before the immensity . . . the elusiveness of the material world . . . that escapes us just when we think we have got hold of it . . . the goal that's never attained . . . the insufficiency of the means at our disposal. . . . There are certain pictures, for instance . . . those by Franz Hals when he was already nearly blind . . . or the later Rembrandts . . ." I felt myself being drawn irresistibly onto a slippery incline, I knew that I ought to stop, but I was seized with a sort of foolish daring, perhaps, too, the need I have to defy her, that sort of giddiness that impels certain guilty persons, aware that they haven't a chance, to make a mad

attempt to forestall their adversaries and challenge them
. . . "or let's say . . . for instance . . ." I looked away . . . "there
is a picture . . . you've never seen it, probably, . . . it's not
very well known . . . a portrait . . . in a Dutch museum
. . . it isn't even signed . . . the portrait of an Unknown
Man . . . Man with Doublet is my name for it . . . well,
there's something in that portrait . . . a sort of anguish . . . a
sort of appeal . . . I . . . I prefer it to anything else . . . there's
something uplifting. . . ." I looked at her: it seemed to me
that she was watching me with a serious, keen expression
that I had never seen her wear before; she looked away,
she seemed to be staring at something in the distance, but I
felt that she was looking inside herself, and she smiled
softly—the sort of embarrassed, amused, touched smile
that people have sometimes when you bring up in their
presence certain intimate and slightly ridiculous recollections of their early childhood. All at once I felt stirred by
an outpouring of gratitude and hope . . . that timid, tender
gleam, the affectionate light in her eye, I watched it alight
and loiter willingly over a mental picture within herself,
the one that I saw inside myself, the same that she had doubtless recognized in me a while back, when she had looked at
me so closely; we both looked at it, it was the picture of a
narrow vestibule . . . in the threatening silence furtive
noises could be heard. . . . They were behind the doors,
waiting . . . there was not a moment to lose . . . open the
door, open the door quickly, look here papa . . . she had
hold of the doorknob and was turning it as gently as possible, she was whispering, leaning against the keyhole . . .
for goodness sake, open the door, it's ridiculous, people can
hear us. . . . If he didn't open, something was going to

happen, something final, something sure and hard, everything was suddenly going to petrify, take on rigid, heavy outlines, they were going to spring triumphantly forth wagging their heads, relentlessly: "So you see, what did we tell you, he's an egoist and a miser. . . ." But he wouldn't allow that, she knew it well, they both knew it well, he was going to open the door . . . she would see him again, as she knew him, as she had always known him, not the cheaply manufactured puppet, the dime-store trash intended for the common herd, but as he was in reality, indefinable, without outlines, soft and warm, malleable . . . he was going to open the door for her, he was going to let her in, nothing ever happened between them, nothing ever could happen between them "for good," their games would go on, huddled up close to him, she would feel once more their secret pulsation, weak and gentle as the palpitation of still warm viscera.

Yet no . . . in reality I had never believed all that, I had never been wrong about it, way down deep inside, I had been expecting it, I had never stopped watching for it, the hardly perceptible shudder of disgust which she gave now all of a sudden, the slightly shrinking gesture she made. She turned to look at me once more with an inscrutable, hard expression that repulsed me and kept me at a distance. Condescendingly she smiled: "Ah! yes, so that's it . . . that's what I thought. . . . The way you judge painting. . . . You are just as you always were. . . . Incorrigible. . . . Watch out, that's very unhealthy; nothing good ever comes of it, that . . ." she pronounced her words with a sort of repugnance . . . "that sort of too personal contact . . . the pursuit of emotions of that kind. . . . If I were you, I should be careful. I don't need to tell you, nothing is more dangerous"—she spoke as though reluctantly, between clenched teeth, with a disgusted expression, as though she were obliged to rub up against something repugnant—"there's nothing more detestable than to mix things that don't belong together." As though in a dream, I heard a faraway voice call out: "Ladies and gentlemen, it's time to leave." She gave a start and looked at her wrist watch with an air, suddenly, of near joy: "Oh, my goodness, I have an engagement downstairs at a quarter to five. They must be waiting for me already. Excuse me. I must run." She took my hand, which I hadn't the strength to lift, shook it hastily and left.

I had a strange sensation, a sort of faintness, a slight dizziness. I took a few steps and dropped down onto the bench in the middle of the room, which was beginning to empty. The people in the crowd that flowed slowly by in front of me looked relaxed and satisfied, even replete. They glanced at me absent-mindedly without seeing me.

When had I had this sensation before, this same harrowed feeling of the contrast between the satisfied indifference of all these strange faces and my own distress, my forlornness? I know. It was on a bare public square, all gray, or else on a wide boulevard bordered with dusty trees . . . I was very small and had wandered away. I had lost my parents and was trying to find them among the Sunday crowd that strolled peacefully along without paying any attention to me. At times I thought I recognized something familiar and reassuring in the line of a back or the cut of a coat, and I would run. . . . But what was I doing there wasting my time, there was not a second to lose, I must hurry right away, catch up with her and, taking hold of her gently by the elbow, watch her turn around, watch her once more, just once more. . . . But it was too late, she must have been gone by then. And yet there might still be a chance. I sprang up, hurried through the crowd, knocking into people, and ran to the window, looking. . . . There she was, I saw her right away, that thin, dark silhouette of uncertain age, walking along beside the wall. I saw her slightly flattened back, her long stiff legs sheathed in black, the swinging of her arm carrying the schoolbag, and beside her—I hardly dared believe it—was he, I recognized his long dark overcoat, his stooped back, one shoulder higher than the other, his rather short neck, his biggish head topped with a gray felt hat . . . and yet it seemed to me that there was in his general aspect, in his entire bearing, something strange that I did not succeed in defining very clearly; perhaps, in the lines of his back, something a bit stiff, a bit stale, like a sort of platitude or banality: a difference, in any case, from the picture I had retained of him, as subtle as the difference one sometimes succeeds in detecting with such difficulty between a cleverly made copy and its original. Now there was nothing—or was it I who had changed?—nothing about him, as formerly, that was at once aggressive and shifty, and that had gripped me so strongly; on the contrary, he was spreading himself there before me with a sort of complacency, with calm indifference. His haunches, a little broader or lower, swayed back and forth, displacing the air at each step with a regular movement, to the right then to the left, with quiet satisfaction and imperturbable self-assurance. It seemed to me that she was walking in step with him; she had the same slightly loose gait: they advanced without hurrying, displacing the air from each side, swaying with the same movement. Little by little the two silhouettes, at the end of the street, became nothing more than a single dark spot. I stuck my neck out as far as I could, I pressed my cheek to the windowpane to watch her until the last, until she had disappeared around the corner.

*I*t was that back—those heavy haunches
spreading out on either side of the chair with an almost insolent expression of satisfaction and self-impor-
tance, that had suddenly arrested my eye. And only then—
as in one of these picture puzzles in which we first discover
the form of an ear or an eye hidden in the lines of a landscape, or a tree, or a house, and then, all at once, thanks to
this clue, the entire animal, I saw them, as well: she and
the old man, seated against the wall, on the far side of the
table.

It was not to be wondered at that I had not recognized
them at first—and yet they had probably been there for

some time, like myself, they had finished their lunch and were drinking their coffee. Nor was it to be wondered at that I had not noticed them, they had changed so much, and through a curious mimetism, had become so indistinguishable, fitted in so exactly with the commonplace, flashy, restaurant dining room, with its mirrors, polished brass, potted plants and bright red velvet seats: flat, highly colored images, similar to those that surrounded them, to all the people eating lunch, seated about them at the other tables.

She particularly was almost unrecognizable. A gray suit. Bright-colored scarf. Hair piled smartly on top of her head in great puffs. Even a bit made-up: her round face—she had put on weight, her face had filled out—had that smooth, flawless look, that sort of set glamor, that make-up gives.

As for the old man, I couldn't see him entirely. I only had a glimpse of his shiny pate and of one of his heavy dewlaps, congested until it was almost purple, protruding over his stiff collar.

The man seated opposite them had pivoted in his chair in order to attract the attention of the waiter. Turned to one side, with his legs crossed and one elbow leaning on the table, I had a three-quarter view of him. A "monsieur" who was neither old nor young, and rather stout. His light brown, somewhat reddish hair, already sparse on the temples, was sleeked straight back with care. The skin of his heavy-featured face was a purplish pink and appeared a bit moist, as though pickled. It seemed to me that everything about him, including the style of his clothes, was vaguely reminiscent of the old man. Same cut. Same sort of Sunday-best look. Same stiff collar and pearl stickpin. And, on his foot, shod with a soft, pointed, black kid shoe, which he dangled nonchalantly, a certain protuberance which I seemed to have noticed also on the old man's foot—a bunion, I believe that's what it is called—just at the base of the big toe. Comfortably seated, leaning slightly backward and swinging his foot, he spread himself before me with a certain bumptiousness. Extremely sure of himself. Unperturbed. Imposing. A rock. A cliff that has resisted all the onslaughts of the ocean. Unassailable. A compact block. All smooth and hard.

Just as people who have little confidence in their own impressions, or are uncertain of what they know, keep looking in their guidebook to see what to think when they're sight-seeing in a foreign city, I too, in his presence, kept casting about for help, for points of reference, as my eye lighted, all at sea, now on his nose with its widespread nostrils: a sign—I seemed to remember—of insolence . . . or was it sensuality? now on his thin-lipped mouth: also sensuality. . . ? or was it thick lips that revealed this. . . ? and yet, I had been told that often thin lips, too, contrary to what people thought . . . at times, on his undershot jaw: self-willed? stubborn? arrogant? . . . at others, on his rather low forehead: narrow minded? however, those two bumps are supposed to denote intelligence . . . or again I would catch his eye in which there seemed to glow the contented quietism that accompanies agreeable digestion. . . . Ineffectual, childish efforts, feather-light darts that bounced against him without penetrating, as harmless as the sticks with which children load the guns that come with their soldier outfits.

I saw that they, too, had finally noticed me. She had been the first to see me and had pointed me out to her father, in a low voice, without lifting her eyes. Now they were looking at me, nodding and smiling, making signs for me to come and join them. Their companion also looked at me in a manner that was devoid of curiosity, quiet and, on the whole, kindly disposed.

Not a trace of trembling on my part. Not the slightest discomfiture. No jumping, either backwards or forwards. No hesitation. Persons in a state of hypnosis, when they carry out movements they are ordered to make, must have this same sensation of supernatural ease and assurance that I experienced as, under the spell of this gaze that was filled with calm confident expectation, I rose as I was supposed to do, crossed the room with a self-assured step, neither slowly nor hastily, and approached them with a broad, cordial gesture of my outstretched hand and a good-natured smile on my face: "Well, well. . . ! and how are you? It seems an age. . . ." I looked at her. . . . "May I say that you're looking extremely well. . . ." Their companion rose—he was rather tall, taller than I am, and somewhat stout—she introduced him with a timid, proud smile. . . . "You don't know each other?" She blushed: "This is my fiancé. . . ." Her father completed the introduction: "Get acquainted. . . . This is my future son-in-law: Louis Dumontet. . . . Do sit down. . . ."

Monsieur Dumontet stepped aside to let me pass. I sat down in the chair beside him.

My eye fell upon a number of papers and sketches spread out among the empty coffee cups. The old man's eye had followed mine: "As you see, we are very busy making plans . . . you may have some ideas on the subject. . . . Maybe you can help us. These young people want to do over a country place. . . ." Monsieur Dumontet laid his large, fleshy hand, the very white freckled hand of a red-haired person, palm down on the papers; with a slight shrug he pursed his lips in an expression of unpretentiousness: "Oh! it's just a little place I own not far from Paris. An old hunting lodge with a bit of land, that I inherited. But I've never lived there. I've kept it more as an investment than anything else. At that, however, it's worth more than paper. But now" —he looked at her, smiling at her—"I thought it might be fixed up. . . . The country around it is pretty, not far from the Oise. . . . Perhaps you're familiar with it . . . between Hédouville and Beaumont?" In my mind's eye, I examined the region closely. . . . Hédouville . . . Beaumont. . . . "Is it Persan-Beaumont, on the Pontoise line?"—"That's it. Exactly. You get off the train at Champagne, the station before Beaumont. . . ."—"Ah! yes, I see where you mean . . . I know it. . . ."—"You do see it? you follow the road towards Hédouville, the one that runs across the plateau. . . ." My inner eye, still on the alert, was docilely following his lead. "A road with lots of hairpin turns that goes up through a field? then through a wood?" Monsieur Dumontet encouraged me. "And there you are. Around three kilometers to the right. . . . You see it, perhaps. . . . A small village. . . ." I saw it. I was there, I had arrived. Much pleased with his look of approbation, I retrieved: "A few houses . . . a square tower?"— "That's right. You certainly do know that neighborhood well. . . ."—"I should say I do. An uncle of mine had a place near Persan and I used to go there often during vacations. He used to take me fishing. . . ." Dumontet turned facing me and looked at me with great interest: "Ah! so you like to fish. . . . In that case, you'll understand me. For me, the great charm of that region is the fishing. Only, when it meant going all alone. . . . Now, on Sundays, I'll be able to go and tease the fish a bit. . . . What did you catch, pike? And how? Trolling?" I tried to remember: "No, my uncle used live bait."—"Ah! trolling is much better, especially in a river like the Oise. You'll see, when we're settled, you must come and see us one day, I'll show you. . . . Only, that's not all . . ." he looked at them, at her and at the old man . . . "there's still a good deal to be done . . . we were just about to. . . ." In a corner, at the bottom of one of the papers, I began to examine the detailed plans of a house: "So that's the house? But, I say, at present that must be quite a job to restore all that. Are there many repairs to be made?"—"Still a good many. The house. . . ." With the end of his fat forefinger with its broad close-clipped nail, Dumontet tapped a circle drawn in the center of the plan. The three of us leaned towards it. . . . "The house—except for a part of the roof— is not in too bad condition. But there's one thing. . . . We have some rather ambitious plans, we should like to make it a little more comfortable, electricity has already been put in, but there should be running water, at least in the kitchen. We should even like, eh . . . ?" He looked at her, smiling and winking one eye, the way we look at a child to whom we're about to give something nice . . . "if there is enough room on the lower floor, we should even like to put in a bathroom. . . ." I felt something glide by, something pass, hardly a pale glow, a hardly perceptible crackle . . . she looked at the old man . . . something in her quivered . . . the old man's voice was slightly hoarse: "A bathroom? A bathroom?" Dumontet stared at him calmly with his cold eye. It seemed to me that I saw a slight note of irony, the ghost of a smile in his stare. . . . "Why, of course. . . . And why not? You know, actually, it's an investment that's as good as any other . . . it changes the value of the house." The old man raised his eyebrows, pursed his lips and shook his head slowly with an air of doubt: "Oh! as for it being an investment, if I were you . . . don't count on it too much. Before you'll be able to get back all you've spent. . . ."

She looked at Dumontet with an expression of confident expectation and pride. Dumontet seemed to be thinking. He lowered his eyelids as though to increase the sharpness of his vision. At the very end, on the fine point of his glance, I seemed to see the house entirely renovated, entirely furnished, and, just off the kitchen, supplied by the same waterpipe—it only meant making a hole in the wall, a short pipe was all that was needed—the shiny little bathroom, the porcelain washbasin, medium-sized, with nickel-plated faucets, and then, beside this picture, a roll of bills, or else a figure written on a piece of paper at the bottom of a long column: 145, the estimate submitted by the Pontoise contractor. 150, all finished, with the price of the hot-water heater. Dumontet's glance changed its direction. It lighted now on the old man: a picture with clear outlines—not a shadow; not a crinkle; shining: as though petrified—came to replace the porcelain tub and the nickel-plated faucets. . . . Dumontet was explaining in his calm, well-poised voice: "Not at all. Don't say that. Do you know what a house like this one, with modern comforts, is worth today? You don't know? Well, I can tell you. Out of curiosity, I asked the local notary." He leaned over towards the old man: "500 grand, at the very lowest. And without counting the land." The old man lifted his head, as though somebody were pulling it, by short jerks, from down to up: "Ah? Ah? are you sure of that? Five hundred thousand francs? As much as that . . . ? In that case, in that case, then, I have nothing more to say. My first impression was that it was a lot to spend on a house that, when all is said and done, will be lived in very little." She assumed the tone of a very good little girl. "Oh! papa, don't say that. We'll be going there often. And during the summer vacation . . . Louis has three weeks' leave . . . next year, when he gets to be assistant director, he will even be able to take a month. . . ." She was a frisky, puffed up ball—like a tamed bird that has just taken a nice dust bath on the edge of its little metal tub, and is shaking its ruffled feathers. . . . Safe at last. Out of harm's way. The old man had gone a bit too far with her and she had been really scared. . . . Now, however. Look. All over. Not a breath. Not a quiver. Nothing had happened. We could skip it. Dumontet and his Medusa look. Everything grew petrified. Dumontet was speaking: "Such is life, eh . . . ? And you know, if you think about it, 150,000 francs, at 3 per cent, makes an annual rent of hardly 4500 francs." He gave a sly little laugh: "That's better, don't you agree, than to squander money in certain business ventures. . . ."

Now it was the old man's turn to wrinkle his lids, he appeared to be counting: "4500 francs rent. . . . You'd have to call that 4500 francs additional rent. That's somewhat different. And it's not a mere trifle, just the same. . . . Anybody can make mistakes, naturally, but don't say that, even today it is still possible to make investments that pay better than 3 per cent." I looked at her. She didn't appear to be listening. Her face showed nothing now except that expression of confident absence that they wear—one had only to look at all the faces of the women seated at the neighboring tables—that air of peaceful, vague rumination that they take on while the men beside them talk business or discuss figures.

Dumontet's hand was resting on a corner of the plan. He turned to his future father-in-law: "Oh, by the way. It's settled. I bought that piece of land. The one I told you about. That big field. It starts here, look,"—our eyes riveted to his finger we followed the line—"and stretches up this way as far as the woods. That gives us about seven acres of farm land. Oh! naturally, it's not as rich as the richest. The soil is chalky, just as it is in that entire region. But if it's well fertilized, in two or three years. . . . My tenant farmer. . . ." The old man looked dumbfounded: "Your tenant farmer? You've got a tenant farmer?" I too showed a certain amazement: "A tenant farmer, so they do tenant farming in that region? I didn't know that." Dumontet leaned back in his chair, as though a bit annoyed, thrumming the table. "No, actually, they don't. It's more of a Southern custom. Only, I was able to arrange it. I came across a former gardener whom I shall allow to live in the house. For the first three years, everything that is produced will belong to him. There's no other way to do it. The land is entirely fallow, and a lot of work will be needed to put it in good condition again. After three years, we'll divide." The old man appeared to be fidgeting slightly, to be gently kicking in his seat: "You'll share the produce? But how will you be able to tell whether you've really received your share?" I seemed to perceive a slight jigging on her part, too. She looked anxiously from her father to her fiancé: "Yes, Louis, do you know him well enough? Because he'll be left with everything . . . the entire house. . . ." Dumontet pressed both hands against the edge of the table and tilted his chair back, the better to see her. He wore an amused smile: "Ah! indeed. . . . Of course he'll be left with the house. In fact, he'll be there to do just that, to take care of it. Believe me, you can put your mind at rest, take my word for it. He's a very decent man. He worked as caretaker in the same place for fifteen years . . ." he might have been stroking her gently, giving her nice little pats on the back. . . . "And you know . . . as for the kitchen, don't worry, it's all arranged. I warned him. He won't set foot in our part of the house. He's going to get his meals on a sort of charcoal stove in the barn." She let him continue, rubbing up against him, all soothed and delighted: "Oh! Louis, did you ask about the apple trees?" Dumontet laughed: "Ah! the apple trees, that's true. . . ." Smiling, he appealed to me: "Now, isn't that just like a woman. . . ." All the fidgeting and thrumming had disappeared as though by magic: in myself the frightened little animals, the swift little serpents, had fled; I nodded, amused, laughing. Dumontet looked at her fondly: "Well, my dear, in that connection, I'm sorry to say, I have some bad news for you. We won't make that apple jelly this year. Nor next year. I inspected the whole orchard with the tenant. Most of the trees are dead. And the others will need to be treated. I told him to buy some saplings. . . ." The old man gave a hearty laugh: "Ho-ho-ho. . . . So you're going to plant

216

trees? You're going to plant apple trees? Well, boys and girls, believe me, I'll never get a taste of those apples." Dumontet: "Of course you will. Why not? You certainly will. . . . With good saplings in that kind of soil, six or seven years from now. . . ." I: "Apple trees are the principal trees of that region. My uncle used to make cider that was as good as the best Normandy cider." Dumontet: "Ah! cider, we certainly shall make some too. But the gardener has advised me especially to plant winter apples." We kept it up for a long time. Dumontet: The Daughter: The Father: I: Dumontet: The Father: The Daughter: Cider apples. Winter apples. St. Laurence apples. Red Roller apples. Goose-foot apples. . . . Not a sound now. Not the slightest spark between them, or between them and me. Not a trace of a current. Dumontet had us all well in leash and was leading us with a sure hand. We came back to the purchase of the land: "And what are you going to plant? Clover? Colza?"—"Ah no, not in that kind of soil. Potatoes —that's what's usually planted to begin with. The tenant will furnish the fertilizer. As I told you, he's a very valuable man. He can buy it very cheaply."—"Natural fertilizer: it seems there's none better." Watching attentively we follow, like well-trained musicians who know their score by heart. Fishing. Hunting. Walking. Frémincourt. The Isle-Adam woods. Nesles-la-Vallée. Beaumont. Not a second of inattention. Never the slightest absent-mindedness. And even, in my case, not a trace of stiffness. Or lassitude. No. Not so long as he was there. Finally Dumontet stopped. He stretched a bit and, with a sigh, took out his watch: "All this is very fine. . . . But now, eh, dearie—he looked at her —I think we'll have to be leaving. Aunt Bertha is expecting us at three. And it's a long way off. . . ." Dumontet turned to me: "I have a cousin who is an architect. He's going to help me a bit, and give me some advice." The old man seemed admiring and amazed: "An architect? Already? You do work fast. . . . So you really have made up your mind about it all?" Dumontet: "Certainly, I have. Oh! I'm not the kind that likes to let things drag along. With me, it's no sooner said than done." The old man smiled good-naturedly. "Fine. Fine. Well, children, you'd better get going. . . ." They rose. I held out my hand to Dumontet: "Well, Monsieur Dumontet, I wish you good luck." Dumontet shook my hand: "Thanks, thanks a lot. And I hope you'll come and see it all when we get settled. I'll take you fishing. And you'll see"—he shook his finger—"you'll come around to my opinion, once you've tried it, you'll never do it any other way. You'll see: trolling is the only way to catch pike."

It was over. They were gone. I sat down again opposite the old man. I don't know what it was that still had the power to upset me—it could only be the result of a habit of long standing, something rather like a conditioned reflex—I don't know what made me suddenly feel once more, as I glimpsed, in the mirror opposite, the reflection of their backs going through the revolving door for the last time, a sort of vague nostalgia, the ghost of a wrench.

We sat there without moving, the old man and I, facing each other. He seemed all shrunken, as though played out, and his face had drooped a bit. I must have looked that way, I, too, must have had that same abandoned look when

I dropped down like that onto the bench, at the exhibition. They had outsmarted him, too. He, too, had been faced with a too powerful opponent. Perhaps he had gone too far with his game, had tempted fate too much. Or perhaps his partner hadn't been up to his level. In any case, no matter how hard you try, as I had done, to put all the odds in your favor, to take every precaution, the unforeseen always happens. The game is too dangerous. The contrivance you are trying to manipulate explodes in your hand.

I saw him smiling at me. He pointed to the empty seat beside him: "Come and sit over here, you'll be more comfortable." At this gesture of perfectly simple and slightly absent-minded kindliness on his part, I experienced the same pang, the same pity, that I had felt years ago, when I seemed to notice in my parents' indulgence and unaccustomed gentleness towards me, the first signs of old age. I no longer felt, as I used to, that he was palpating and probing me in order to discover my most sensitive spot. There was nothing left in me that excited him, or even incited him to try to provoke me. No matter how closely I listened, I could no longer catch the old resonances in our conversation, the old echoings and reechoings that used to plunge so deep down inside us. Harmless, anonymous remarks, noted down long ago. They reminded one of old gramophone records. As we sat there side by side on the wall sofa, we probably looked like two big dolls that have just been wound up: "Yes, indeed, how time flies. . . . It's an age since we last met . . . I often wanted to get in touch with you, and then the time passed . . . one doesn't know how . . . time passes too fast . . . and we get older every day, don't we, we're getting old all right. . . . Making way for the next generation. . . ." He paused for a moment as though something in him had jammed, then he started up again. . . . "Well, you saw that, eh, my daughter's getting married. . . ?"—"Yes, indeed. . . ! I hadn't heard . . . I was agreeably surprised."—"Well, such is life! but it's none too soon. . . . She should have been thinking about her future a long time ago. . . . After all, I'm not going to last forever. It's high time somebody took my place. . . . Oh, I did the best I could, I brought her up as best I could, and it wasn't always easy, it's hard for a man alone. Because, you know, she's not always so good-natured as she might be, she's got a temper of her own, but anyhow, I hope everything will go all right now, I believe she's done pretty well for herself. . . ." It seemed to me that everything he was saying had an unreal ring to it. I wondered if he believed it himself, entirely, or if he had the impression of reciting something that he felt forced to repeat. But this was surely nothing but the inability I always have to accept what is evident, to believe that things have "really happened"; my reluctance to follow sincerely the road to recovery, that my specialist spoke of. . . . He, the old man, had taken it in— he always did take things in more quickly than I did—he knew that there was no other way out and he was resigned. Perhaps he was trying now to lend me a hand, and show me the way, to help me take the step. . . . "As for that, you probably saw for yourself . . . my future son-in-law is not in the prime of youth, either, eh. . . ? But these marriages of convenience between persons getting on in life. . . ." Nodding as though in spite of myself, I completed his sentence for him: "Are often the best of all." Now it was his turn to nod: "Yes, indeed. . . . For that matter, he's a serious-minded chap, and he's not badly off. He has succeeded in putting a little money aside. He's a man of simple tastes. And the fact is, I can't give them very much. I may live quite a while yet, you have to plan for everything. I've always done everything I could not to depend on anybody in my old age. . . ." I nodded respectful approval: "Certainly . . . I can understand that. . . ." As we talked I began to feel a slight nausea, a certain giddiness . . . but it was probably nothing serious . . . it would pass. Just a hard step to be taken, and afterwards everything would go better. All that was needed was to let myself be guided without giving a thought to anything, to answer submissively the way I was doing, nodding judicious assent. . . . "Oh, certainly, things won't always be rosy. . . . They'll have to be careful, as I always was." I continued to approve, I understood. . . . "But as for that, I believe he's quite steady in his ways, he's a chap who started with little, and he's always worked hard. And my daughter, too, for that matter—what else can you do?—has always been made to take a serious attitude towards life. . . ." These words, which he seemed to reel off quite mechanically, must, after a while, have had the same soothing, exorcising power that the simple monotonous words of prayers have on the faithful: it suffices at times only to recite them mechanically in order to resist the temptations of the evil one, or to strengthen a faith that is waning. Little by little faith will return. One has only to submit. Rely on them in all humility. Now that I had gone so far on the right path, they would not abandon me. I would find help on every side. That was all they expected, I knew it; they asked only to welcome me. Thus the Church welcomes generously her strayed lambs and opens wide her arms to her repentant children. They were expecting me. I had only to come.

The women with the rather faded, slightly washed-out faces, who air themselves in the doorways of the big apartment houses with the blighted façades, or else in the wan little squares, will not grow silent now when they see me coming. They will know right away—they are never wrong—that they need distrust me no longer, that I am one of them.

I shall sit down beside them without fear, on the dusty benches, right up against the box hedging. They will wag their heads and look at me with their placid eyes: "Believe me, it's much better like that. . . . I always hoped, poor thing, that she would find a good husband. And she was lucky in her misfortune. You can certainly say that it was a piece of unhoped-for luck for a reliable, serious-minded gentleman like Monsieur Dumontet to want to marry her, because they say that her father gave her next to nothing. He decided it was too good an opportunity to get rid of her, and at little cost to him. . . . Oh! he never forgets to figure things out: what an egoist, what a miser, you don't see many like that. . . . Of course, when you know him . . . in his home, the way I know him . . . I can tell you a lot about him, believe me, I worked for them for twenty years. . . ."

Piously, I shall mingle my voice with theirs. . . .

Little by little everything will grow calm. The world will take on a smooth, clean, purified aspect. Somewhat akin to the air of serene purity that the faces of people are always said to assume after death.

After death. . . ? But that, too, that is nothing, either. Even that rather strange look, as though things were petrified, that slightly lifeless look, will disappear in time. Everything will be all right. . . . It will be nothing. . . . Just one more step to be taken.

Paris, 1947